My Secret Unicorn

Twilight Magic
and
Friends Forever

Two exciting adventures in the
My Secret Unicorn series
together in one bumper book!

*

Have you ever longed for a pony? Lauren
Foster has. When her family moves to the
country, her wish finally comes true. And
Lauren's pony turns out to be even more
special than she had ever dreamed.

My Secret Unicorn

Twilight Magic
and
Friends Forever

Linda Chapman

Illustrated by Ann Kronheimer

PUFFIN

PUFFIN BOOKS

Published by the Penguin Group

Penguin Books Ltd, 80 Strand, London WC2R 0RL, England

Penguin Group (USA) Inc., 375 Hudson Street, New York, New York 10014, USA

Penguin Group (Canada), 90 Eglinton Avenue East, Suite 700, Toronto, Ontario, Canada M4P 2Y3
(a division of Pearson Penguin Canada Inc.)

Penguin Ireland, 25 St Stephen's Green, Dublin 2, Ireland (a division of Penguin Books Ltd)

Penguin Group (Australia), 250 Camberwell Road, Camberwell, Victoria 3124, Australia
(a division of Pearson Australia Group Pty Ltd)

Penguin Books India Pvt Ltd, 11 Community Centre, Panchsheel Park, New Delhi – 110 017, India

Penguin Group (NZ), 67 Apollo Drive, Rosedale, North Shore 0632, New Zealand
(a division of Pearson New Zealand Ltd)

Penguin Books (South Africa) (Pty) Ltd, 24 Sturdee Avenue, Rosebank, Johannesburg 2196, South Africa

Penguin Books Ltd, Registered Offices: 80 Strand, London WC2R 0RL, England

puffinbooks.com

My Secret Unicorn: Twilight Magic first published 2006
My Secret Unicorn: Friends Forever first published 2006
First published in one volume 2008

2

Text copyright © Working Partners Ltd, 2006
Illustrations copyright © Ann Kronheimer, 2006
All rights reserved

The moral right of the author and illustrator has been asserted

Typeset in Bembo by Palimpsest Book Production Limited, Grangemouth, Stirlingshire
Made and printed in England by Clays Ltd, St Ives plc

British Library Cataloguing in Publication Data
A CIP catalogue record for this book is available from the British Library

ISBN: 978-0-141-32514-9

www.greenpenguin.co.uk

Penguin Books is committed to a sustainable future
for our business, our readers and our planet.
The book in your hands is made from paper
certified by the Forest Stewardship Council.

My Secret Unicorn

Twilight Magic

'Goodness,' said Mrs Wakefield. 'You should feel very honoured, Lauren. Apart from me, you're the only person Apple has approached since Currant's been born. You must have a real way with horses.'
Lauren felt a glow of pride. Jessica and Mel grinned at her but Jade looked cross that Lauren was getting all the attention . . .

To Poppy and Kitty Young

CHAPTER

One

The night air felt cool against Lauren's arms as she ran down the dark path to Twilight's paddock. Above her, the stars were twinkling brightly in the clear sky.

A perfect night for flying, Lauren thought. She smiled. She was so lucky! Although Twilight, her pony, looked just like any other small grey pony, he was really a unicorn in disguise. Every night when Lauren said the magic Turning Spell he changed into his true form and then he could talk, do magic and fly.

Lauren knew Twilight wasn't the only secret unicorn. In fact, there were unicorns disguised as ponies all over the world. Each unicorn was supposed to find a special human friend to help them change into their magical shape and then they did good deeds together. Lauren and Twilight had helped lots of people and animals since she had first found out that he was a unicorn.

Tonight there was someone else who needed their help. Lauren speeded up. What would Twilight say when she told him her plan?

Twilight whinnied as she ran up to the gate.

'Hi, boy,' Lauren panted. 'We've got a

job to do tonight!' She quickly said the
Turning Spell.

'*Twilight Star, Twilight Star,*
Twinkling high above so far.
Shining light, shining bright,
Will you grant my wish tonight?
Let my little horse forlorn
Be at last a unicorn!'

With a bright purple flash, Twilight's grey coat became snow-white, his mane and tail grew and shone silver in the starlight and a long horn appeared on his forehead. He was a unicorn once again!

'Hello, Lauren,' he said, nuzzling her. 'Does someone need our help?'

'Yes. It's Buddy,' Lauren replied. Buddy was her brother Max's Bernese mountain dog. 'He's really miserable because Max has gone to stay with some friends who live in the city. He's never been away for more than a night before, and Buddy is missing him so much! He won't eat or play or do anything.'

'I thought he looked quiet when I

saw your dad taking him for a walk today,' Twilight said. 'But what can we do to help him?'

'I thought you could tell him that Max will be home in a few days,' Lauren explained. 'I don't think he understands that Max has just gone on holiday; I think he's afraid that Max has gone away forever. If you could tell him what's happening, maybe he'd feel happier.'

Twilight nodded. 'It's worth a try. But is it safe to let him see me when I'm a unicorn?'

'I was wondering that,' Lauren admitted. Until now she and Twilight had been careful not to let Buddy see Twilight in his magical shape in case the dog started acting strangely around Twilight. No humans were allowed to know about Twilight's secret, and Lauren didn't want to risk her parents or Max finding out. 'But Buddy's not a puppy any more. I'm sure if we explain that he mustn't let anyone know your secret, he'll understand that he has to act as if you're just an ordinary pony.' She sighed. 'I know it's a bit risky but I really want to help him.'

'Me too,' Twilight agreed. 'Let's do it!'

Lauren ran back to the house. Twilight had said just what she was hoping he would.

Buddy looked up from his bed when she came into the kitchen but he didn't woof. He was used to Lauren creeping in and out of the house at night.

'Come on, Buddy,' she whispered.
'Walk!'

Usually Buddy leapt around madly at
the prospect of a walk but now he just
got heavily to his feet and walked over.
He licked Lauren's hand in a subdued
way. He really wasn't his usual bouncy
self at all. Hoping her plan would work,
Lauren took hold of his collar and led
him out of the house.

When Buddy reached the field and
saw a unicorn standing by the fence, he
stopped dead and tilted his head to one
side, looking very surprised.

'It's OK, Buddy,' Lauren soothed
him. She climbed over the fence and

Buddy followed her, shuffling under the railing.

Twilight snorted in greeting and touched Buddy with his horn. 'Hello, Buddy. It's just me, Twilight.'

Buddy's ears pricked up as he looked at Twilight curiously.

'I'm a unicorn,' Twilight told him.

'But you mustn't let anyone know. Not even Max.'

At the mention of Max's name, Buddy's ears and tail drooped. He whined miserably.

Twilight understood what he was saying. He could talk to all kinds of animals when he was a unicorn, and they could talk back to him. 'No,' Lauren heard him say to the young dog. 'You've got it wrong. Max hasn't gone away forever, Buddy. He's just on holiday for a few days. He *is* coming back.'

Buddy's ears pricked up again. He barked, and to Lauren it sounded just as if he was saying 'Really?'

'Yes,' Twilight promised. 'Max will be

home in just a few days.' He glanced at Lauren. 'You were right. Buddy *did* think Max had gone forever.'

'Oh, Buddy,' Lauren said, ruffling the dog's fur. 'Max would never abandon you. He loves you.'

Twilight repeated her words to Buddy.

'Woof!' Buddy barked. Suddenly he looked like a different dog. Bounding away, he stopped and crouched down, wagging his tail.

'I think he wants us to play chase!' Twilight said.

Lauren grinned. 'What are we waiting for?'

She ran after Buddy with Twilight trotting beside her. With his mouth open

wide in a doggy grin, Buddy raced in
circles around them.

At last Lauren stopped, puffing and
out of breath. 'OK, come on, Buddy,' she
said. 'Time to take you back inside.'

Giving a quiet woof goodbye to
Twilight, Buddy trotted beside Lauren

up the path. When they reached the kitchen, he ran over to his bowl and polished off the biscuits he had left earlier. Then he lay down in his bed with a contented sigh.

'See you later, boy,' Lauren whispered, shutting the door.

Happiness glowed through her as she ran back to the field. She loved using Twilight's magic to help people and animals. Having a unicorn was just great!

'Thanks for explaining things to Buddy,' she said to Twilight as she climbed over the fence. 'I'm so lucky to have you.'

'I'm the lucky one,' Twilight said. 'You're a wonderful unicorn friend.'

'Me? I don't really do anything,'

Lauren protested. 'It's your magic that solves things.'

Twilight looked at her in surprise. 'That's not true. You do just as much as me.'

'No, I don't,' Lauren said modestly.

'You do,' Twilight insisted. 'Think of what happened tonight. I talked to Buddy but it was your idea. You were the one who realized that he needed someone to explain things to him.'

'I suppose so,' Lauren said slowly.

'You're very special,' Twilight told her.

Blushing, Lauren changed the subject. 'Are you looking forward to tomorrow? It's going to be fun, isn't it?'

Twilight nodded and swished his tail.

The next day Lauren had arranged to
meet up with her two best friends, Mel
Cassidy and Jessica Parker. They were
going to ride over to Orchard Stables, a
local livery stables which was owned by
the mother of their friend Grace. One
of her mares had just had a foal and
Lauren, Mel and Jessica were going to

go and see it. Afterwards they were going to take a picnic lunch to the creek.

'I can't wait to see Currant,' Lauren told Twilight. 'That's what Grace and her mum have called the foal.' She smiled. 'I'm glad it's the holidays – we'll be able to visit him lots. As well as doing all kinds of other fun stuff, of course.'

Twilight pushed her with his nose. 'How about we start by going flying?'

'Cool!' Lauren said. Taking hold of his mane she scrambled on to his back. 'Let's go to the woods and jump over the tree tops.'

Twilight soared into the air. 'Sounds good to me!'

CHAPTER

Two

The following morning, Lauren was
fastening Twilight's girth when she
heard the sound of hooves. Turning, she
saw Mel and Jessica riding towards her
on their ponies, Shadow and Sandy.

'Hi, Lauren! Are you ready?' Mel
called.

'Almost.' Lauren checked Twilight's
girth was tight, and mounted. 'Have you

brought your lunch?' she asked, riding over to meet them.

Jessica patted a saddlebag behind her leg. 'Yep, here it is. Shall we go through the woods or across the fields?'

'Across the fields,' Lauren said. 'It's much quicker.' Orchard Stables bordered on to Lauren's dad's farm and he had said it was fine for them to ride around the edges of the fields.

As they rode down a tractor track, Lauren looked around at the ears of young spring wheat waving in the breeze. Overhead the sky was blue and the sun was shining. She sighed happily. 'Isn't it great to be riding instead of being at school?'

Mel nodded. 'No maths, no dumb projects. No more Jade Roberts!'

Lauren grinned. Jade Roberts was in their class at school. She was always boasting about the prizes she had won on her pony, Prince. She used to tease Mel because Shadow hadn't been a very good jumper. That is, until Lauren and Twilight secretly helped him to overcome his fears. What's more, Jade had once owned Twilight but she'd sold him to the Fosters because she didn't think he was showy enough. *Luckily for me*, Lauren thought, stroking Twilight's mane. Jade hadn't cared enough about Twilight to find out his magical secret!

Then she forced herself to push all thoughts of Jade out of her mind. It was far too nice a day to think about someone who was so annoying! 'Shall we canter?' she called to the others.

'Yes!' they replied together.

They clicked their tongues and the three ponies surged forward eagerly.

With the breeze blowing in their faces,
the girls cantered towards Orchard
Stables.

The yard seemed very busy when they
arrived. There were people everywhere,
carrying rugs and tack and leading
ponies.

'I wonder what's going on,' said Mel.

'Let's ask Grace,' Lauren said, seeing a tall slim girl with blonde hair hurrying out of the barn with a stack of buckets. She waved.

'Hi!' Grace called. Dumping the buckets by the water trough she came over. 'Have you come to see Currant?'

Lauren nodded. 'If it's still OK.' She glanced around. 'It looks pretty busy around here.'

'There are six new liveries arriving today,' Grace replied. 'Fox Run – the livery stables on the other side of town – is closing down and quite a few of the owners have decided to bring their horses here. It's great for Mum to have the

business but it does mean it's going to be
crazy today. Mum's in the tack room
sorting things out and I've been trying to
make sure the loose boxes are ready.'

'Do you want a hand?'
Jessica offered.

Grace smiled.
'Thanks. It
would be
great to have
some more help.'

Lauren, Mel and
Jessica tied their
ponies to a hitching rail and followed
Grace to the tack room. There was
stuff everywhere! Rugs, saddles, bridles
and grooming kits were piled up all

over the floor. Grace's mum was
sorting through them with Jo-Ann,
Grace's best friend.

'Hello, girls,' said Mrs Wakefield. 'If
you've come to see Currant, I'm afraid
you'll have to wait a while. I have to
get this tack room sorted out first.' She

ran a hand through her short blonde
hair. 'It could take some time!'

'Would you like us to help?' Lauren
said.

Mrs Wakefield's face lit up. 'That
would be very kind, thank you!'

'What should we do?' Mel asked.

'If you could take the rugs into the
rug room and hang them up for me that
would be a great help,' said Grace's
mum.

Lauren, Jessica and Mel set to work.
With three of them working together
it didn't take long. Soon the rugs were
hanging up tidily in the rug room,
outdoor rugs on one rug rack, indoor
rugs and sweat sheets on another.

Meanwhile, Mrs Wakefield and Jo-Ann had hung up the saddles on saddle racks and sorted out the hats, boots and bandages into piles.

'Here are the last two rugs,' Lauren called, carrying two heavy New Zealand rugs across the yard for Jessica and Mel to hang up.

As they started draping the rugs over the racks, they heard the sound of raised voices outside.

'That stable on the corner is supposed to be for my pony. You'll have to move!'

'But I was here first!'

'Well, obviously no one told you it was reserved for my pony, Prince!'

Lauren's eyes flew to meet Mel's and Jessica's. There was no mistaking that bossy voice.

'It's Jade Roberts!' she cried.

Three

Lauren, Mel and Jessica hurried to the doorway.

Jade was standing in the middle of the yard, glaring at a younger girl. 'Go on, move your pony out so I can put Prince in.'

Looking upset, the younger girl began to lead her pony out of the stable.

Jade smiled smugly. As she turned

away, she caught sight of Lauren, Mel and Jessica. 'What are you three doing here?' she asked.

'We could ask you the same question,' Lauren replied.

Jade tossed back her shoulder-length brown hair. 'I've just moved Prince here. We were at Fox Run until it shut down.'

Lauren's heart sank. That meant if they came to see Grace and Jo-Ann they'd probably end up bumping into Jade as well.

'So, why are you here?' Jade asked them curiously. 'You're not moving your ponies here as well, are you?'

'No,' Jessica answered. 'We just rode over to see Mrs Wakefield's new foal.'

'A foal?' Jade echoed, looking interested. 'How old is it?'

'Just a few days,' Mel replied.

'Cool,' Jade said. 'Where is it? I want to see it too.'

As she spoke, Mrs Wakefield came out of the tack room with Grace. 'Ah, someone else who wants to see Currant,'

she said, smiling. 'Well, why don't you join us, Jade? Now the tack room's done, I can take you all over to the foaling stable.'

'I'll come too,' said Grace. 'Currant's going to be mine when he gets older,' she told them proudly as they headed across the yard.

Her mum nodded. 'That's right. Grace is going to help me break him in.'

'How do you break a horse in?' Lauren asked.

Before Mrs Wakefield could reply, Jade piped up. 'I helped my cousin break in a pony last summer. It was great. I was the first person to ride him because my cousin's seventeen and a bit big for him. You might have heard of my cousin,' she said to Grace and her mum. 'She has eight horses and does lots of show classes with them. Her name's Maggie O'Donald.'

'I have heard of her. She wins a lot.' Mrs Wakefield looked impressed. 'It must have been a great experience for you, helping someone like that break in a pony.'

'It was,' Jade said. 'I know I'm *really* lucky.'

Lauren rolled her eyes at Mel and Jessica. Jade always acted sugary sweet around adults. She only showed her other side when there were no grown-ups around.

'I'm afraid you won't be able to touch Currant and Apple,' Mrs Wakefield warned them as they approached the foaling stable. 'Although Apple, Currant's mum, is usually really gentle, she seems to be feeling very protective of her new baby. I don't want to upset her or risk anyone getting hurt, so you'll just have to look at Currant and not touch him. OK?'

They all nodded.

The foaling stable was a single large stable set on its own, away from the main barns. Compared to the hustle and bustle of the yard it was very peaceful. The door of the stable opened on to a small wooden-fenced paddock.

'Here we are,' Mrs Wakefield announced. 'I'll let Apple and Currant out.'

The girls waited by the fence while Grace's mum opened the stable door and then stepped back out of the way.

After a moment, a dapple-grey mare walked out. She had a dished face, big

expressive eyes and a long grey mane.
She looked around and then whickered
softly over her shoulder. There was an
answering whinny and out of the stable
trotted a tiny black foal, with long
spindly legs, enormous dark eyes and a
tail that stuck straight out like a
bottlebrush.

He stopped beside his mum and looked
curiously at the people by the gate.

'Oh, wow!' Lauren breathed. 'He's
gorgeous!'

'Very cute!' Mel agreed.

Grace looked pleased.

The foal's eyes flicked around. There
wasn't a trace of fear in his expression;
he just looked lively and inquisitive.

'Will he stay black?' Lauren asked, remembering that she'd read somewhere that grey horses were usually born black.

Jade shot her a withering look. 'Of course he'll st—' she started to say at the same time as Grace said:

'We think he'll turn into a grey, don't we, Mum? Black foals usually do.'

Jade hastily corrected herself. 'Of *course* he'll change colour, Lauren.' She made it sound like it had been a really dumb question.

Currant began to walk towards them. As he neared the fence Apple cut in front of him, stopping him from reaching them. She threw her head in the air, as if warning them to stay away.

'She wasn't this protective the first time she had a foal, was she, Mum?' Grace said.

Mrs Wakefield shook her head. 'It's still early days. I'm sure she'll settle down soon.'

Lauren looked at the anxious mare.
'It's all right, girl,' she murmured. 'We
don't want to hurt you or your baby.'

Apple looked at her.

'He's very beautiful,' Lauren told her
softly. 'You must be very proud.'

Apple slowly stretched out her muzzle
towards her. Lauren held out her hand.
Taking a cautious step forward, Apple
sniffed at Lauren's fingers. She blew
down her nose and stared at Lauren
with her big dark eyes.

'Goodness,' said Mrs Wakefield. 'You
should feel very honoured, Lauren. Apart
from me, you're the only person Apple
has approached since Currant's been born.
You must have a real way with horses.'

Lauren felt a glow of pride. She always seemed to get on well with horses, even nervous ones. Jessica and Mel grinned at her but Jade looked cross that Lauren was getting all the attention.

'Well, I'd better be getting back to the yard,' said Mrs Wakefield. 'Stay here as long as you want but please don't try and touch Currant. I don't want Apple to get upset. I'm leaving you in charge, Grace, OK?'

'OK,' said Grace.

Mrs Wakefield headed back to the yard.

'Currant's so cute,' Jade said. She put her hand through the fence. 'Here, boy,' she called.

'Jade, don't,' Grace said quickly. 'You heard what my mum said.'

'Chill out,' Jade said. 'Apple will be fine.' She held out her hand again and clicked her tongue.

'No, Jade!' Grace exclaimed, grabbing her arm. 'Don't be so dumb!'

Jade shook her off. 'I'm not dumb!'

'Well, you're acting that way,' said Grace. She turned to the others. 'Come on. I think we should all go back to the yard. I don't want to risk upsetting Apple.'

'OK,' Lauren said reluctantly. She could see why Grace didn't want to risk staying there with Jade acting the way she was. 'Bye, Apple. Bye, Currant.'

Currant pricked up his ears and suddenly an image flashed into Lauren's mind – a picture of Currant grown up, his coat sparkling white, and a silvery horn on his head.

She stared at Currant's broad forehead and slender legs, at his intelligent face and bold expression. She'd just had an amazing, wonderful thought.

Could Currant possibly, just possibly, be a unicorn in disguise?

CHAPTER
Four

'Lauren, come on!' Mel called.
'Coming!' Lauren shot a last look
at Currant and hurried after her friends.
Her mind was buzzing. Could Currant
really be a unicorn? She knew that
Twilight had been born in a magic land
called Arcadia and that he'd come to live
among humans when he was a year old.
However, she also knew that sometimes

unicorns were born on earth as foals. She couldn't wait to ask Twilight what he thought.

'So how about it, Lauren?' Grace said. 'Are you going to come?'

'Come where?' said Lauren.

'To the Fun Day,' Grace said.

'Fun Day?' Lauren echoed.

'Lauren!' Mel grinned. 'I could tell you weren't listening. Grace was just telling us that her mum is organizing a Fun Day for later this week.'

'It's to help welcome the new people to the stables,' Grace explained. 'There's going to be gymkhana games and a Handy Pony class. Are you interested?'

'Definitely!' A thought struck Lauren. 'But will that be OK? I mean it's not as if we keep our ponies here.'

'It'll be fine,' Grace said. 'Mum wants as many people here as possible.'

'Prince is much too valuable to go charging about in gymkhana games,' said Jade. 'But I suppose I *could* take him in the Handy Pony.'

'Don't force yourself,' Mel muttered. Jade glared at her.

'What happens in a Handy Pony class?' Jessica asked Grace.

'It's a class that tests how safe and obedient a pony is,' Grace explained. 'You have to do things like getting the pony to walk over a plastic sheet, carry a flag, open and shut a gate while you're on the pony, and do a few small jumps. It's really fun.'

'Cool!' Mel said enthusiastically.

They reached the yard. 'I'd better go and see if Mum needs me to do anything,' Grace said. 'If you're not busy tomorrow, why don't you come over in the morning and practise?'

'I can't,' Mel said regretfully. 'I'm going to the dentist.'

'And it's my stepsister Samantha's turn to ride Sandy tomorrow,' Jessica said.

'I can come,' Lauren said.

'All right, I'll see you tomorrow about ten, Lauren,' Grace said, and she hurried off.

Lauren turned to Mel and Jessica.
'The Fun Day sounds brilliant, doesn't
it?'

Jade smirked. 'It's lucky for you there
aren't show classes, Lauren. Twilight's
looking scruffier than ever. Don't you
ever groom him?' She glanced across
the yard to where Twilight was standing.

'Yes, actually, I do − *every day*,' Lauren said shortly. She walked over to Twilight.

'Really? You can't tell,' Jade replied, following her.

'Shut up, Jade!' Mel exclaimed.

'Twilight looks a million times better with Lauren than he ever did when you had him!' Jessica said hotly.

Lauren was grateful for her friends' support but she didn't want to get into a quarrel with Jade. 'Let's go,' she said to Mel and Jessica. 'We can ride to the creek and have our picnic.'

Jade frowned, cross at being ignored. 'Just look at Twilight, Lauren,' she went on loudly. 'His mane needs pulling and he's been rubbing his tail and . . .' All of a sudden Twilight sneezed all over Jade's smart black jacket.

Jade gasped. 'Yuck!' she cried, staring at the sticky mess on her sleeve. 'Look what's he done to me! That's gross!'

Lauren couldn't hide her grin. 'Sorry, Jade. You must have been standing too close, but never mind, I'm sure it'll wash off.'

Twilight tossed his head, his eyes gleaming mischievously. Lauren was sure he'd sneezed on purpose. It served Jade right for making mean comments! 'Come on, boy,' she said, patting his neck. 'Let's go for our picnic!'

★

It was fun eating lunch by the creek and letting the ponies paddle in the water. Spring flowers grew along the riverbank and the trees were green with new young leaves. As Lauren munched on a chocolate biscuit, she felt very happy. It was the beginning of the holidays, she had a fun show to look forward to, and there was a possible new unicorn nearby! Not even the memory of Jade's mean words could dent her cheerfulness. She just hoped that Twilight hadn't been upset by what Jade had said.

Beside her, Jessica sighed. 'We should go home. I said I'd be back by two o'clock.' Getting to her feet, she fed the remains of her apple to Sandy.

'All right,' Mel said, picking up her hat and squashing it on to her black curls. 'Let's tack up again.'

They rode home through the woods and stopped when they reached the end of the track where Lauren needed to turn left to ride back to her farm.

'Should we meet on Wednesday morning and get ready for the Fun Day together?' Mel said.

Jessica nodded and Lauren said, 'I'll come round about eight.'

The girls said goodbye and went their separate ways.

As Twilight began to walk down the track towards Granger's Farm, Lauren looked around. She really wanted to talk to him. 'Come on, Twilight,' she said suddenly. 'Let's go to the secret clearing.'

He turned off the path on to an overgrown track that led through the trees. Lauren had to duck low on his neck to avoid the overhanging branches. The path twisted through the trees until it opened into a clearing. Yellow and white butterflies fluttered through the air and the grass was studded with purple and gold flowers.

Lauren said the Turning Spell.

'Hey, there,' Twilight said as he changed into a unicorn. 'Is everything OK?'

Lauren knew he was wondering why she had turned him into a unicorn in the middle of the day. 'I just wanted to

talk to you,' she explained. 'I'm sorry about what Jade said about you being scruffy. Are you upset?'

'Of course not.' Twilight shook his mane. 'I know I'm not the neatest, most beautiful pony in the world, but I don't mind. The other ponies can't fly!'

'You're the most beautiful pony in the world to me,' Lauren said loyally. She sighed. 'Jade's so annoying.'

'It's best just to ignore people like that,' Twilight said.

'I know.' Suddenly Lauren remembered something. 'Oh, Twilight, I think Apple's foal might be a unicorn!'

'Really?' Twilight looked excited.

Lauren told him all about Currant. 'He seemed so intelligent. Is there any way we can tell for sure?' she asked.

'Not definitely,' Twilight said. 'Foals don't find out if they're unicorns until they're one year old but there are usually some clues. It's just the same way as a

human who might be a possible unicorn
friend can be spotted – because they
have a good heart and believe in magic.
Foals who might be unicorns also have
certain qualities – they're usually very
clever and very curious.'

Lauren pictured the foal with his wise expression. 'I really think Currant might be a unicorn!'

Twilight pricked up his ears. 'Well, why don't we visit him? If I see him I might be able to spot some special unicorn-ness about him.'

'OK,' Lauren agreed. 'Let's go tonight!'

That evening, Lauren and Twilight swooped across the dark fields towards Orchard Stables. Lauren grinned as she thought how surprised the cows would be if they looked up and saw Twilight flying through the sky!

They landed in a copse of trees by the foaling stable and Lauren dismounted. She looked round carefully in case Mrs Wakefield had decided to come and do a last check before going to bed. Grace and her family lived in a house at the other end of the drive leading down to the yard.

Everywhere was quiet, so they walked over to the stable. Apple was lying in the straw with her eyes closed. Currant was on his feet, nosing inquisitively around the stable.

'Currant!' Lauren whispered.

The foal looked up. Seeing Twilight looking over the door, his eyes widened. He stared at Twilight's horn as if he couldn't believe what he was seeing.

Twilight whinnied softly. The foal

walked over and stretched out his velvety nose. Twilight breathed out softly.

'Hello,' Lauren heard him say. 'I'm Twilight. I'm a unicorn.'

Currant whickered curiously.

'Yes, a unicorn's like a pony,' Twilight replied. 'But we have horns on our heads and we can fly and do magic.'

Currant stamped one tiny hoof and snorted.

'What's he saying?' Lauren asked.

'He says he'd like to be a unicorn too.' Twilight turned back to the foal. 'I'm afraid you can't be. At least not yet. But maybe when you're older.'

'Do you think he will be one?' Lauren said.

'I think he might.' Suddenly Twilight tensed. 'Listen!'

'What?' Lauren said.

'I heard a noise outside.' As Twilight spoke, Lauren noticed that his horn had started to shine with a silvery light. 'It sounded like footsteps. Someone's coming!'

'Quick,' Lauren said in alarm. 'We'd better go. Bye, Currant!'

They backed away from the stable. What had Twilight heard? Lauren hoped it wasn't Grace's mum. Suddenly her eyes caught sight of a moving shadow. One of the barn cats was padding down the path towards the stable, making no noise at all on its delicate paws.

'It's just a cat.' She turned to Twilight.
'Is that what you heard?'

'Yes!' Realization dawned on Twilight's
face. 'I *knew* it didn't sound like a
human's footsteps.'

'But how did you hear something so
quiet?' Lauren said, looking at him in
amazement.

'I don't know, I just did,' answered
Twilight, looking puzzled.

Lauren noticed his horn was still
shining, and her stomach flipped
over with excitement. 'Maybe it's a
new magic power!' Twilight had
lots of magic powers but he only
found out about them one by
one.

'Yes!' Twilight agreed. 'Wow!' He looked pleased. 'I've got a new power.'

Lauren stroked him. 'It's a really useful one. We'll be able to use it to hear if anyone's sneaking up on us, or to check if anyone's around when we're flying.'

Twilight nuzzled her happily. 'I like it when we find out about new powers.'

'Me too,' grinned Lauren.

She took hold of his mane and swung herself on to his back. As Twilight rose into the air, Lauren looked down at Orchard Stables. She thought about the next day. It was going to be great to practise with Jo-Ann and Grace. Maybe she'd even get to see Currant again. She pictured the curious foal.

I hope he's a unicorn, she thought excitedly. *I really do!*

CHAPTER
Five

'Hi, Lauren!' Jo-Ann called as Lauren rode in to the yard the next morning. Jo-Ann was grooming her pony, Beauty.

'Hi!' Lauren rode over. 'Is it still OK if I come and practise with you?'

'Of course,' Jo-Ann replied. 'But Grace and I have decided we won't actually enter the competition. Mrs Wakefield wants us

to help steward the classes instead. It's fine
by us because we enter loads of shows
already. It will be fun to help out.'

Just then Grace came out of a stable.
'Hello, Lauren. Are you all ready to
practise for the Handy Pony?'

Lauren nodded.

'I need five more minutes to finish
grooming,' Jo-Ann said.

Grace looked at Lauren. 'Do you want
to come and see Currant while we wait?
You can leave Twilight here.'

'OK.'

Lauren tied up Twilight and followed
Grace across the yard.

Apple was eating some hay by the
paddock gate and Currant was standing

beside her. When he saw the two girls, he came towards the fence, but catching the warning look that Apple shot in their direction, Grace and Lauren stayed back.

'I wish we could stroke him,' Grace said. 'It's not like Apple to be aggressive.'

'I guess she just wants to look after her baby,' said Lauren.

Grace smiled. 'I would too if he was mine. He's gorgeous.'

Currant looked at them cheekily from under his mum's neck, then stuck his muzzle in the pile of hay, and tossed his head, sending hay flying into the air. Lauren and Grace giggled. Currant snorted and then pushed his head under Apple's tummy and started to feed.

'He's adorable!' Lauren said.

Grace smiled. 'He is. Come on, let's go and see if Jo's ready to practise.'

Ten minutes later, Lauren, Grace and Jo-Ann rode into the schooling ring. Grace and Jo-Ann had put out a course that was similar to the Handy Pony competition but not exactly the same, because that would be cheating.

'You have to ride through those cones,' Grace said, pointing out a row of six cones. 'Then pick up that flag and carry it to the bucket. Ride over the sheet of plastic, through the gate and then over the three jumps.'

'I'll go first,' said Jo-Ann. Lauren knew Jo-Ann's bay mare, Beauty, was fantastic at jumping. But she didn't seem to like Handy Pony. She spooked at the cones, knocking two over. She wouldn't go near the flag, and stopped dead when she got to the plastic. Jo-Ann talked to her patiently, and eventually Beauty leapt over it as if it was a jump and charged towards the three fences. She cleared them easily.

Jo-Ann rode back to the others.
'Maybe it's a good thing I'm not
entering the Handy Pony class after all,'
she said with a grin. She patted Beauty's
neck. 'Jumping's more your thing, isn't it,
girl?'

Beauty tossed her head.

'My turn next,' said Grace. Her pony, Windfall, was much steadier than Beauty and he went right round the course, only stopping at the plastic. But after a few coaxing words from Grace he stepped over it.

'Well done!' Jo-Ann called.

'That was great,' Lauren said.

Grace looked pleased. 'Thanks. Take your time with the plastic – ponies are often a bit worried by it at first.'

Lauren gathered up her reins. She had no idea how Twilight would behave because she'd never done anything like this with him before.

Twilight seemed to have worked out

what to do. He trotted calmly around
the cones, being careful not to touch
them, and stopped by the flag so that
Lauren could pick it up. Then he walked
up to the bucket and waited while she
put it down. But he stopped when he
reached the plastic sheet and looked
down at it, snorting.

'Good boy,' Lauren said, squeezing
him on. Twilight put a hoof on the
plastic. It rustled and he hesitated.
Lauren could tell he was worried. An
idea came to her and she dismounted.
Holding on to Twilight's reins she
walked on to the plastic herself.

'Look,' she said. 'It's fine.' Twilight
stared uncertainly at the plastic beneath

her feet. She walked over and stroked his
nose. 'You know I'd never ask you to do
anything that would hurt you. Trust me,
Twilight. It's OK.' Twilight put his head
down and sniffed at the plastic. Then to
Lauren's delight he walked on to it.
'Good boy!' she exclaimed, leading him
across to the other side.

She got back on and this time he trotted over the plastic without hesitating.

Jo-Ann and Grace clapped. 'Well done!'

Twilight flew over the three jumps and Lauren cantered him back to the others.

'That was great!' said Jo-Ann. 'It was a really good idea to get off and lead him over it.'

'Shall we have another go?' Grace suggested.

They had each ridden round the course a few more times when Lauren saw Jade ride into the ring on Prince. Lauren groaned to herself.

'Are you practising for the Handy Pony?' Jade asked them.

Grace nodded.

'I'll practise too,' Jade said. She began
to warm Prince up. It was easy to see
why he had won so many prizes. He
moved with long smooth strides and did
everything Jade asked, going from walk
to trot to canter at the lightest of aids.
Jade was a good rider, although she
seemed very strict, correcting Prince
sharply for the slightest mistake.

At last she started the course. Prince
went brilliantly until he reached the
plastic. He stopped dead about a metre
away from it and stared at it with wide,
scared eyes.

'Walk on!' Jade commanded.

Prince didn't move.

Jade nudged him firmly and when he still didn't move she growled at him. He hesitated and took a tiny step, then changed his mind and ran backwards.

'Just take it slowly,' Grace called.

'I know what to do,' Jade snapped back. She gave Prince a tap with her whip. 'Walk on!'

Jo-Ann jumped off Beauty and handed the reins to Grace. 'Getting cross won't help,' she said, starting to walk towards Jade. 'Here, let me lead him.'

'He can do it!' Jade smacked Prince again.

He leapt forward, landed on the plastic and cantered over it in two bounds.

'There!' Jade said, giving them a

triumphant smile. 'I told you he could do it.'

Lauren glanced at Grace and Jo-Ann. They didn't look impressed.

'Yes, but will he ever go near plastic again?' Grace muttered. She turned to Jo-Ann and Lauren. 'I'm going to take Windfall in now. Are you two coming?'

They nodded. When they got back to the yard, Lauren patted Twilight and dismounted. 'You can have a rest and then we'll go home,' she said.

She gave him a drink and then picked out his feet, being careful to sweep up the mud from his hooves. She didn't want to leave a mess on the yard. She was just putting the broom away when

Jade rode over and tied Prince up next to Twilight.

Lauren went to the tack room and bought a can of lemonade from the drinks machine. When she had finished, she went back to Twilight.

Prince had gone but the place where he had been tied up was covered with bits of mud. Jade had obviously picked out his hooves and not swept up the mess.

Just then Mrs Wakefield came round the corner. She saw the mud and frowned. 'Lauren, could you fetch a broom and clean your mess up please?'

'But the mud's not from Twilight's hooves,' Lauren protested.

'Whose pony is it from then?' asked
Mrs Wakefield.

Lauren hesitated. She didn't like
telling tales. 'Um . . .'

Just then Jade walked round the
corner. 'Lauren! Haven't you cleared up
the mess from Twilight's hooves yet?' She

turned to Grace's mum, her eyes wide. 'I told Lauren we have to clear up after ourselves here, Mrs Wakefield.'

Lauren stared at her in outrage. 'But it's not Twilight's mess!'

'It is,' Jade insisted. 'I saw you picking his feet out.'

'Yes, I did, but I swept the mud up!' Lauren exclaimed. 'It's –'

'OK. Enough!' Mrs Wakefield interrupted them. 'I don't know who made the mess but Lauren, seeing as Twilight is tied up here, would you mind getting a broom and clearing it up for me?'

Lauren nodded glumly. Jade shot her a triumphant grin.

'And Jade,' Mrs Wakefield went on, 'I'd like you to help Lauren.'

'But –' Jade started to protest.

'*Please*,' Mrs Wakefield repeated in a steely voice.

Lauren had a feeling Jade hadn't fooled Grace's mum after all.

Jade seemed to decide not to argue. 'Sure, Mrs Wakefield,' she said, smiling sweetly.

When Grace's mum walked away, Lauren turned crossly to Jade. 'It was your mess all along!'

Jade smirked. 'And now *you've* got to clear it up.'

'You mean *we've* got to,' Lauren said through gritted teeth. 'I'm going to get some brooms.'

She marched over to the barn and fetched two brooms, but when she returned, Jade had gone. The mess, of course, was still there.

Lauren felt like screaming. Could anyone be more annoying than Jade Roberts?

CHAPTER
Six

'Lauren, could you pass the shampoo, please?'

'Sure. Here it is!'

It was the morning of the Fun Day and Lauren, Mel and Jessica were grooming their ponies at Mel's. Lauren scrubbed at Twilight's grass stains with warm soapy water. She wanted him to look as beautiful as possible. She wasn't going to give Jade any opportunity to criticize him.

A picture of Twilight in his unicorn form flashed into her mind. If only Jade knew what he really looked like! Lauren grinned as she imagined how jealous Jade would be if she knew that Twilight was a unicorn in disguise and that Lauren was his unicorn friend. The night before, she and Twilight had spent several hours swooping through the forest while he had practised using his new power of magical hearing. He'd told her everything he could hear as they had flown through the trees – the squeak of a tiny mouse, the rustle of a grey squirrel in the branches of an oak tree,

the whine of a fox cub as he waited for
his mother to return. It had been great
fun. Lauren put her arm over Twilight's
neck and gave him a hug. She, for one,
was very glad that Jade wasn't his
unicorn friend!

Next to Twilight, Jessica was washing
Sandy's white socks and Mel was putting
a tail bandage on Shadow. 'I wonder
how we'll do in the classes,' Lauren said
to them.

'Well, I hope we beat Jade after what
she did to you yesterday,' replied Mel.
Lauren had told her friends about Jade's
trick.

'I don't care what she does,' Lauren shrugged. 'I'm just going to ignore her.'

'Me too,' Jessica agreed, and Mel nodded.

When the ponies were gleaming, the girls went to get changed. Lauren had decided to wear her cream jodhpurs and brown jodhpur boots. She didn't have a riding jacket but it was just a fun show so wearing a shirt and jumper would be fine. She braided her hair in a neat plait and put on a pair of black gloves that she had been given for Christmas. They had her name embroidered on the cuffs in small white writing and looked very smart.

I look just fine, she thought, examining her reflection in Mel's bedroom mirror.

She turned to the others. 'Are you ready?'

'I am,' Mel said, jumping up from the bed where she had been putting on her socks.

'So am I,' said Jessica.

Lauren grinned. 'Then let's go!'

A huge banner hung over the gate that led to Orchard Stables. *'Orchard Stables Fun Day!'* it announced.

'Wow!' Lauren exclaimed. 'Doesn't the yard look great?'

There were balloons tied to the gates and strings of paper flags looped over the barn doorways. A refreshment table had been set up at one side of the yard. There were plates of sandwiches, delicious-looking chocolate brownies, and a cake stand piled high with white and yellow cupcakes. A big sign read, 'Please help yourself and don't forget treats for your horse!' An arrow underneath pointed to two buckets, one filled with carrot pieces and one with horse biscuits.

'I vote we head over there,' said Jessica, looking hungrily at the cakes.

'Let's go and put our names down for the classes first,' Lauren said.

They rode towards the table where Jo-Ann and Grace were taking entries for the classes.

'Shall I enter for all of us?' Lauren asked.

'OK,' Mel replied. 'I'll hold Twilight.'

'Hi, Lauren!' Grace called. 'Which classes do you want to enter?'

Lauren grinned. 'Everything!'

Grace started scribbling Lauren's, Mel's and Jessica's names on to the entry sheets. There was going to be a sack race, a flag race, a walk, trot and canter race, and the Handy Pony competition. 'Mum's got a secret idea up her sleeve for the Handy Pony,' Grace told Lauren. 'She always likes thinking of new twists to classes. I like your gloves, by the way,' she added.

'Thanks,' Lauren said. 'I got them for Christmas.' She broke off as she heard a familiar voice.

'You're in my way! I'm trying to get to the gate! Move!'

Jade was riding through the other
ponies towards the gate. Prince's dark bay
coat was gleaming and his two white
socks were spotlessly
clean. Jade was
wearing a smart
black showing jacket
and white
jodhpurs.

She caught
sight of
Lauren. 'I see
you decided
not to dress
up, Lauren.'

Lauren flushed.

'You look fine,' Grace reassured her.

'It's just a Fun Day. There'd be no point in dressing as if you were going to a huge big show.'

Jade frowned.

Just then Mrs Wakefield lifted a loudhailer. 'Please could all the entrants for the gymkhana games come to the ring!'

Lauren hurried back to Twilight. It was time for the Fun Day to begin!

A starting line was marked out with cones at one end of the schooling ring. A row of sacks had been laid out for the first race. Lauren, Mel and Jessica rode into the ring with about fifteen other people. Mrs Wakefield explained that she was going to split them into four groups for each race. The winner of each group would go through to a final to decide the rosettes.

All the races were great fun. There was lots of shouting and laughing as people got tangled up in their sacks, tripped over and dropped flags.

By the time the races were over, Twilight was no longer looking neat and tidy. His mane was sticking up, his legs were speckled with mud and he had damp patches on his neck, but Lauren didn't care. They were having a wonderful time and that was all that mattered!

She rode out of the ring with two rosettes – a second place in the sack race and a third in the walk, trot and canter.

Jessica won the walk, trot and canter, and Mel came third in the flag race and fourth in the sack race.

'Wasn't that cool?' Mel exclaimed as they rode out of the ring, rosettes fluttering on the ponies' bridles.

'It was brilliant,' Lauren agreed.

Jade was sitting on Prince just outside the ring. She looked as though she thought games were too silly for words.

'I think Jade's forgotten this is supposed to be a *fun* day,' Jessica joked.

Lauren and Mel giggled.

In the ring, Grace and Jo-Ann were helping Mrs Wakefield to set up for the Handy Pony competition.

'What do you think Mrs Wakefield's

secret idea is?' Jessica said warily.

'I don't know,' Mel mused. 'The course looks just like Grace and Jo-Ann said it would.'

Mrs Wakefield called the twelve Handy Pony competitors into the ring. 'I thought I'd give all of you riders an extra challenge in this class,' she said with a smile. 'This is supposed to be a day for getting to know each other – and each other's ponies. So instead of this being a Handy Pony class, it's going to be a Handy Rider.'

Lauren glanced at Mel and Jessica. They looked as confused as she was.

'Which means you're going to swap ponies,' Mrs Wakefield went on.

Several people gasped.

'You'll ride someone else's pony around the course,' Grace's mum explained. 'It will be interesting to see how quickly you can form a new partnership with a strange horse. I'll give you all ten minutes to get to know your new ride.' She held up a hat with some pieces of paper inside. 'I've put all your names into this hat. I'm going to ask half of you to pick out a name and then you'll swap with that person. So who wants to go first?'

'I'll go,' Jade said. She fished into the hat and picked out a name.

'Whose name have you got?' said Mrs Wakefield.

Lauren's heart
skipped a beat as
Jade's eyes met hers.
'Lauren Foster,'
Jade announced.
'I'm going to
be riding
Twilight.'

CHAPTER
Seven

Lauren gasped.

'OK, Lauren and Jade swap ponies,' said Mrs Wakefield. 'Someone else's turn to choose a name.'

Jade led Prince over. 'I can't believe I've got to ride Twilight while you get to ride Prince,' she hissed. 'It's not fair. You'll do really well because Prince is brilliant compared with Twilight.'

'Twilight's just as good,' Lauren said angrily. Shooting Twilight an apologetic look, she handed his reins to Jade. He nudged her with his nose as if to say that he didn't mind.

Jade swung herself on to Twilight's back. Not even bothering to pat him, she rode away and began cantering around the ring.

Lauren decided to take a moment to get to know Prince. 'Hi, boy,' she murmured, patting him. 'I'm Lauren.'

Prince was a very handsome pony with a dished face and big dark eyes. He lifted his muzzle to her face and blew out. Lauren knew it was his way of saying hello.

She stood there for a few minutes, talking quietly to him. On the other side of the ring, Jessica was getting on to a pony called Lemonade, while Mel had a stocky skewbald called Ziggy.

'Ride around for a few minutes to get to know your new pony and then we'll start,' Mrs Wakefield called.

Lauren quickly realized that Prince was very well schooled and eager to please. *No wonder Jade does so well on him*, she thought, as they jumped a small cross-pole.

'What's he like to ride?' Mel asked, trotting up on Ziggy.

'Fantastic,' Lauren replied, smiling. She watched Jo-Ann lay a piece of plastic sheeting next to the practice fence. 'I'm going to take Prince over that. He didn't seem to like it much yesterday.'

She rode Prince towards it, aware that Jade was watching her closely. Prince hesitated when he saw the plastic and then stopped. Lauren coaxed him gently with her voice but he wouldn't move.

'You'll need to be firmer than that if
you want to get him to walk over the
plastic,' Jade called.

Lauren ignored her. 'Come on, boy,'
she said. Prince still wouldn't move so
she did what she'd done the day before
with Twilight and dismounted.

'I can't believe you're getting off,' Jade
said scornfully. 'Don't you know
anything about horses? You have to *make*
them do what you want – show them
who's the boss.'

Lauren continued to ignore her. After
a lot of patting and talking to him
encouragingly, she got Prince to walk
over the plastic. At first he jogged
nervously, lifting his hooves high, but

after Lauren had led him over it three times he began to calm down. Lauren mounted and Prince let her ride him across it without a fuss.

'Good boy!' Lauren praised him.

Jade scowled.

'OK, everyone!' Mrs Wakefield called. 'It's time for the first competitor, Jessica Parker riding Lemonade.'

Jessica rode into the ring. Lemonade was a long-legged steel-grey pony who looked quite excitable. He fidgeted with the reins and jogged, but Jessica rode him very patiently and he only made a few mistakes – knocking over one of the cones and refusing to stand still at the gate while she closed it.

'Well done, Jessica. That was a very good round,' announced Mrs Wakefield. 'Now for our second competitor, Lauren Foster riding Prince!'

Prince trotted neatly through the cones and halted by the barrel. Lauren picked up the water bottle but as she was carrying it towards the second barrel it slipped through her fingers and she

had to dismount to pick it up. She heard
Jade laughing from the gate. Red in the
face, she remounted. The rest of the
round went much more smoothly.
Prince stood like a statue while Lauren
opened and shut the gate and although
he hesitated as they approached the
plastic, he walked over it without a fuss
when Lauren patted his neck. He cleared
all three jumps easily at the end.

'Good round, Lauren!' Mrs Wakefield
called as everyone clapped. 'Next we
have Jade Roberts riding Twilight.'

As Lauren rode out, Jade hissed,
'Prince only did well because I've
schooled him! You shouldn't think it was
anything to do with your riding.'

Shortening her reins, she pushed
Twilight into a trot. Twilight tucked his
nose in, looking uncomfortable. Lauren
usually rode him with a very light
contact. But he was very well-mannered
and halted squarely by the barrels and
the gate.

As Jade rode him up to the plastic
sheet, she gave him a tap on his
shoulder with her whip. Twilight swished
his tail in protest but walked over the
plastic. However, from the way his ears
were laid back, Lauren could tell that he
wasn't impressed with being smacked for
no reason.

Jade turned him towards the jumps.
'Canter on!'

Lauren saw a mischievous look suddenly cross Twilight's face. Jade sat down in the saddle and tried to push him into a canter but Twilight just slowed down.

Jade's heels flapped and she smacked Twilight again but it had no effect. He slowed to a jog and then to a walk.

Reaching the first jump, he stopped right in front of it.

A few of the spectators giggled. 'I think Twilight's doing it on purpose,' Mel whispered. 'You can tell from his face.'

Lauren had to agree. There was a very cheeky look in Twilight's eyes.

Jade raised her whip. Suddenly Twilight leapt over the fence from a standstill.

'Whoaa!' Jade cried, her arms flailing. As Twilight landed on the other side, she fell forwards on to his neck. For a moment Lauren thought Twilight was going to put his head down so that Jade would slither off. But he didn't. Instead he lifted his neck and slid her safely back into the saddle.

Jade wasn't hurt and everyone burst out laughing. But Jade didn't see the funny side. Grabbing the reins, she yanked at Twilight's mouth and lifted her whip again.

'Jade!' Mrs Wakefield exclaimed, starting to walk towards her.

Lauren was quicker. Throwing Prince's reins to Mel, she raced across the ring. 'Stop it, Jade!' she shouted.

Jade swung herself off Twilight's back. 'You're welcome to him. He's a useless pony and you're a useless rider, Lauren Foster!'

'He is *not* useless!' Lauren exploded.

'He is. He's —'

'That will do, Jade,' said Mrs Wakefield. 'Lauren, maybe you'd better take Twilight in.'

Lauren nodded. She rubbed Twilight's nose. 'You're *not* useless,' she told him shakily.

'No, he's not,' said Mrs Wakefield, giving him a pat. 'Only bad riders ever blame

their horse, Jade,' she said. 'I think you
need to go and cool down for a while.'

Red in the face, Jade marched away.

'OK,' Mrs Wakefield said. 'Jade
Roberts has retired on Twilight. Can we
have the next competitor in the ring,
please? That's Lindsey Huston on Rusty.'

Lauren led Twilight out of the ring.
'Are you OK?' she murmured. 'I'm
really sorry I let Jade ride you.'

He pushed her with his nose and gave
her a cheeky sideways look.

Seeing the mischievous glint in his
eye, Lauren felt a glimmer of relief. She
had a feeling Twilight was saying he
thought Jade was even more sorry!

As soon they got out of the ring Mel,

Jessica, Grace and Jo-Ann surrounded them.

'Poor Twilight,' said Jessica, stroking him.

'Jade's such an idiot!' Mel exclaimed.

'I couldn't believe it when she almost hit him,' said Grace.

Lauren caught sight of Jade walking past with Prince's saddle. It was obvious she'd heard the comments. Her face went white and, biting her lip, she hurried away.

Lauren hesitated. The last thing she felt like doing was comforting Jade, but she also knew how horrid it was to hear yourself being talked about.

Twilight nudged her with his nose and Lauren realized he'd seen Jade too.

She made up her mind. 'Can you hold
Twilight for a minute?' she said to Mel.

Lauren caught up with Jade at the
tack-room door.

Jade swung round. 'What do you want?'

'I . . . I just wanted to say I'm sorry
you heard that stuff the others were
saying,' Lauren said awkwardly.

'Yeah, right!' Jade spat. 'You think you're so cool, with all your friends telling you how wonderful you are, don't you, Lauren? Well, you'd better watch out. People might not be thinking you're so great for much longer.'

Dumping her saddle on a rack, she marched off.

Lauren stared after her. What had Jade meant? Feeling uneasy, she walked back to the others.

'Where did you go?' Mel asked, handing her Twilight's reins.

'Nowhere,' Lauren said. Not wanting to think about it any more, she said, 'Come on, let's go and watch the rest of the Handy Pony.'

CHAPTER

Eight

The Handy Pony competition finished without any more drama. Lauren was placed third for her round on Prince. Mel came second for an almost perfect round on Ziggy, and Jessica was fifth.

'You've all done really well today,' Grace said to them.

'It's been fantastic,' Mel said happily.

'Yeah,' Jessica agreed, patting Sandy. 'Everyone seemed to enjoy themselves.'

Apart from Jade, Lauren thought. 'Can we see Currant before we go?' she said out loud.

'Sure,' Grace said. 'Come on.'

They tied the ponies up and left their hats and gloves in a pile, then set off towards the foaling stable. As they were passing the water trough, they met Grace's mum. 'Are you going to see Currant?' she asked.

When they nodded, she said, 'Well, be very careful of Apple. She seemed very restless this morning. Don't go into the stable.'

'We won't,' they promised.

Mrs Wakefield smiled. 'Thank you. I know I can trust all of you.'

As she turned to walk away, Lauren noticed Jade standing by the trough. She had a strange expression on her face.

A shiver of unease ran down Lauren's spine. She was sure Jade was planning another mean trick. Trying not to worry about it she headed after the others.

Currant and Apple were in their stable. Apple was lying down and Currant was curled up next to her. When the girls looked over the door, Apple got to her feet and stood protectively over Currant.

'It's all right, beauty,' Lauren murmured. 'No one's going to hurt you.'

The dapple-grey mare's ears flickered.

'She seems to like you, Lauren,' said Grace.

'She does but I bet she's still not going to let us close enough to see Currant,' Jo-Ann said. 'Come on, let's go back to the yard.'

Lauren was reluctant to leave. Apple did seem to be responding to her.

Maybe if she could keep talking to her for a bit longer, the mare would calm down.

The others were already heading up the path. 'Come on, Lauren!' Grace called.

'Coming!' Lauren ran after them.

When they reached the ponies, Lauren, Mel and Jessica began to put their hats and gloves back on.

'Where's my right glove?' Lauren said.

'It must be here,' Jessica said in surprise.

They searched around but there was no sign of it anywhere.

'Don't worry,' said Jo-Ann. 'I'm sure it'll turn up.'

Feeling upset, Lauren got on to
Twilight. She couldn't believe she'd lost
one of her new gloves the first time
she'd worn them.

'Don't worry,' Jessica said, seeing
Lauren's face. 'Your glove's bound to
turn up. No one would steal it. After all,
who'd want a glove with *Lauren Foster*
written on it?'

'I suppose that's true,' Lauren said, feeling a bit more cheerful. She patted Twilight's neck and, sitting back in the saddle, she let him walk on a loose rein all the way home.

That night, Lauren's parents had friends over for supper. As soon as all the adults were settling down at the dinner table, Lauren crept outside. She wanted to talk to Twilight about the show.

'Wasn't Jade impossible today?' she said when she had turned him into a unicorn.

'A bit,' Twilight admitted, nuzzling her arm. 'But I think she got more than she bargained for when she picked me for the Handy Pony. And maybe it will stop her being mean to you,' he added hopefully.

'I doubt it.' Lauren frowned. She told Twilight what Jade had said afterwards. 'She made it sound like she was planning on doing something horrid.' Not wanting to think about it any more, she changed the subject. 'I wish I hadn't lost my glove today.'

'We could always go back to the stables and have another look for it,' Twilight suggested. 'Everyone will have gone home by now.'

'I guess we could,' Lauren agreed. 'You could land by Currant's field and wait in the trees for me. We could take your

saddle and bridle, then if I do meet
anyone, I'll just say I rode you over
there.'

'Good idea,' Twilight said.

Lauren hurried to get her tack. It was
a bit strange to tack Twilight up when he
was a unicorn — she never usually used a

saddle and bridle on him when he was in his magical form. She had to unbuckle the bridle to get it on over his horn.

When he was ready, they flew across the fields. The yard was in darkness, with the only light coming from the Wakefields' house at the end of the drive.

'It doesn't look as if there's anyone around,' Lauren whispered as Twilight swooped towards the trees by the foaling stable.

'I can use my new hearing power to check!' Twilight said excitedly.

He landed on the grass at the edge of the trees and concentrated hard. Lauren saw his horn start to glow with a silver light.

Suddenly Twilight stiffened. 'I can hear someone's voice!' he said in surprise.

'Do you think it's Mrs Wakefield?'

'I don't know. It sounds like a girl. It sounds as if she's saying, "go away".' Twilight listened hard and then looked at Lauren in alarm. 'Whoever it is, I think she's in the foaling stable and it sounds like she's in trouble!'

'In the foaling stable!' Lauren gasped.

'I can't go over there like this,' Twilight said. 'You go and have a look.'

'OK.' Scrambling off his back, Lauren raced over to the stable. As she got nearer she could hear a frightened voice.

'Go away, Apple! Please, go away!'

Lauren stood on tiptoes and looked through the window. Apple was standing with her ears flattened and her neck stretched towards a person who was cowering against the wall.

Lauren gasped. It was Jade!

CHAPTER
Nine

Apple snapped her teeth, missing Jade's arms by millimetres. Jade pressed against the wall with a frightened cry. She was holding something, but Lauren couldn't make out what it was.

Lauren ran back to Twilight. 'It's Jade!' she panted 'She's in the stable and can't get out. We've got to help her. Can you talk to Apple? Persuade her to leave Jade alone?'

Twilight shook his head. 'If I do that Jade will see me. Maybe you should go and get Mrs Wakefield.'

'There isn't time,' Lauren said desperately. 'Apple is really upset.'

'Then *you'll* have to help,' Twilight said.

'Me?' Lauren exclaimed. 'But what can I do?'

'Well, you can't talk to Apple like I'd be able to,' Twilight said, 'but you're really good with horses. You might be able to calm her down, or at least distract her enough so Jade can escape.'

Lauren wasn't sure. She knew Apple was only trying to protect her tiny foal, but she'd looked so fierce!

'You can do it, Lauren,' Twilight urged.

'But . . . but . . .' Lauren stammered.

Twilight touched her face with his muzzle. 'You *have* to do it, Lauren. Jade could get hurt.' He lowered his horn. As it touched Lauren's shoulder, she felt strength and courage flowing into her.

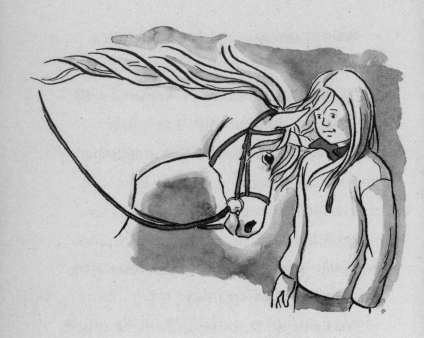

'OK,' she said, taking a deep breath. 'I'll try.'

'Turn me into a pony first,' Twilight told her. 'Then if you need help I can do something without anyone seeing me as a unicorn.'

Lauren quickly said the Undoing Spell. As Twilight turned back into a pony he nudged her with his nose and pushed her gently towards the stable.

Heart pounding, Lauren ran across the grass.

'Lauren!' Jade gasped as Lauren opened the door.

Apple tossed her head at Lauren. 'It's all right, girl,' Lauren murmured. She knew that horses picked up on emotions very easily so it was important she didn't appear frightened. 'Jade's not going to hurt Currant.'

Apple stared suspiciously at her.

Lauren edged into the stable. 'Easy now.' She turned sideways, hoping it would make her seem less threatening.

'Hurry up, Lauren!' Jade exclaimed.
'Get me out of here!'

Apple tensed.

'Be quiet, Jade!' Lauren said. 'I'm
trying to help but you need to stay
calm.'

Outside the stable, Twilight whinnied
encouragingly.

Knowing he was there made Lauren
feel better. Twilight would never have
suggested she try and calm Apple if he'd
thought she wouldn't be able to do it.
I'm not going to let him down, she thought
determinedly.

She looked at the mare. She needed
to distract Apple so Jade could escape.

Lauren felt in the pocket of her jeans
and found a half-eaten packet of mints.

Moving slowly, she pulled out the
packet. 'Here, Apple,' she murmured.
'Yummy mints.' She held out her hand,
making sure she didn't look directly at
the mare. She'd read in one of her pony
magazines that looking straight at a
frightened horse would scare it even
more.

For a long moment nothing happened.
Suddenly the straw rustled as Apple took
a step towards her. A second later, Lauren
felt Apple's muzzle tickle her hand.

'Good girl,' Lauren murmured as
Apple crunched up the mint.

Moving very slowly, she took another

mint from the packet. 'When I say so,
walk very quietly out of the stable,'
Lauren whispered to Jade.

'OK,' Jade said faintly.

Lauren held out the second mint.
Apple came closer and crunched it up.

'Now!' Lauren whispered to Jade.

Jade started to edge along the wall.
Apple immediately pinned back her ears
and swung round. Jade froze.

'It's OK, Apple,' Lauren murmured.
Her heart was thudding but she forced
herself to sound calm. 'Here you go,
have another mint.'

She rustled the wrapper. Apple
lowered her head and turned back to
Lauren. With a sigh of relief, Jade
escaped through the stable door.

Lauren fed the last mint to Apple and
then backed out of the stable. Shutting
the door behind her, she leant against it
for a moment, feeling shaky. Twilight
stepped forward and pushed his head
against her. Lauren stroked him with a

trembling hand. Twilight couldn't talk to
her because he was in his pony form,
but she knew he was telling her she'd
done really well.

Jade was sitting on the ground,
looking very white.

'Are you all right?' Lauren asked.

Jade nodded.

'What were you doing in there?'
Lauren said. 'You know we've been told
not to go into Apple's stable. And why
were you here when it was dark anyway?'

Jade's face flushed and her fingers
curled over the thing she was holding in
her hand. It was black and looked like it
was made of material. Lauren saw some
white writing at the edge.

'What's that?' she demanded.

Jade looked guilty. 'It's . . . well, it's your glove.'

'My glove!' Lauren echoed in astonishment.

'Yes. I picked it up when you left it in the yard today.' Jade bit her lip. 'I . . .

I was going to leave it in the stable so that Mrs Wakefield would think you'd been in there with Currant.'

'What?' Lauren exclaimed. Beside her, Twilight snorted and stamped his hoof angrily.

Jade hung her head. 'I wanted you to get into trouble,' she muttered. She looked up and saw the shock on Lauren's face. 'I'm sorry. I really am. Thank you for rescuing me, Lauren. You were amazing with Apple just now.'

Lauren was stunned. How could Jade have planned to do something so mean? She would have been in real trouble if Mrs Wakefield had found her glove in the stable.

'So why were you here?' Jade asked.

'I wanted to look for my glove.'
Suddenly Lauren noticed that Twilight
was scraping at the ground with his hoof
as if he was trying to tell her something.
A second later, she heard the sound of
someone walking down the path.

A torch swept through the darkness.
'Who's there?' Mrs Wakefield's voice
called sharply.

'It's Mrs Wakefield!' Jade gasped.

Lauren stared at her in alarm. 'Oh no!
What's she going to say when she finds
us here?'

CHAPTER
Ten

Mrs Wakefield walked towards the stable. When the beam of her torch landed on Lauren and Jade, she stopped. 'What are you two doing here?'

'I . . . er . . . well . . .' Jade stammered.

'Yes?' Mrs Wakefield prompted.

'Well, I came to the stable because . . .' Jade looked down at the glove in her

hand and swallowed. 'Because . . .' Her
voice trailed off.

'I'm waiting for an explanation,' said
Mrs Wakefield, face frowning.

Lauren thought hard. She knew
Grace's mum would be very angry if she
learned the real reason for Jade's visit to

the stable, and despite what Jade had
done, Lauren didn't want her to get into
that much trouble. 'You came because
you offered to help me find my glove,
didn't you, Jade?' she said. She didn't like
lying to Mrs Wakefield but it was the
only way to help Jade.

Jade looked at Lauren in surprise.

'I called Jade,' Lauren went on. 'I
wanted to know if she'd seen my
missing glove. Jade said she thought she'd
seen it near Apple's stable and offered to
come and help me look for it.'

Jade shot Lauren an intensely grateful
look. 'Yes, that's right. And . . . and we
found it, didn't we?' She held up the
glove.

Lauren nodded.

'I see,' Mrs Wakefield said slowly. She didn't sound convinced, but to Lauren's relief she didn't question them further. 'Well, you shouldn't have come back here at night-time on your own.'

'We're sorry,' Jade said.

'Yes. It won't happen again,' Lauren promised.

'There's no harm done, I suppose,' said Grace's mum. 'But you two had better go straight home now. Will you be all right on your own, Lauren?'

'I'll be fine,' Lauren answered. 'It's only ten minutes away and Twilight knows the way really well.'

'How about you, Jade? How did you get here?' Mrs Wakefield asked.

'On my bike,' Jade replied.

'Have you got lights for it?'

'No,' Jade admitted.

'Then I'd better run you home in my car,' said Mrs Wakefield. She went to the door and looked over it. 'At least Apple and Currant seem OK. Come on, let's go, Jade.'

'See you soon,' Lauren said to Jade.

'Yes,' Jade said, and for the first time ever she gave Lauren a warm smile. 'Thanks, Lauren. For *everything*,' she added in a low voice.

Lauren smiled back. There was no way Jade would ever be a friend like Jessica or Mel, but maybe their days of being enemies were over. She had a feeling that Jade wouldn't be mean to her or Twilight again soon. 'See you,' she said, and she led Twilight towards the trees.

When Mrs Wakefield and Jade had left, she turned him back into a unicorn.

'What did you think of all that?' she exclaimed.

'I can't believe Jade was going to leave your glove in the stable,' Twilight said.

'I know. I found it hard to decide whether to help her when Mrs Wakefield was asking her why she was here,' Lauren admitted. 'Part of me didn't want to, but I didn't want her to get into loads of trouble either.'

Twilight nuzzled her. 'You did the right thing. I think she'd had enough of a shock already.'

'Yes,' Lauren agreed. She frowned as she thought of the mare. 'Apple seems so upset at the moment. I know she's only trying to protect Currant but it's not like anyone is going to hurt him. I wish we could make her understand that . . .' She broke off as an idea flashed through her mind. 'Hang on. Maybe you . . .'

'Maybe I could talk to her!' Twilight exclaimed at the same time.

Lauren grinned. 'That's just what I was going to say.'

They went back to the stable. When Lauren opened the door, Currant and Apple turned their heads in alarm. Seeing Twilight looking like a unicorn, Currant gave a whinny of recognition and trotted over.

Lauren tensed as she waited for Apple to shoo him back. But Apple didn't. To Lauren's surprise, she whinnied and blew down her nose at Twilight. He greeted her in the same way.

Apple whickered softly.

'What's she saying?' Lauren demanded.

'That she was expecting me,' Twilight said, looking surprised.

Apple whickered again. 'Oh, I understand now,' said Twilight. He turned to Lauren. 'Ever since Currant was born, Apple has been waiting for a unicorn to visit. It's because she thinks Currant might be a unicorn foal — just like we do.'

'Is that why she's been extra-protective?' Lauren asked.

'Yes. She's afraid someone might try and hurt him or take him away from her.'

'Oh, Apple,' said Lauren. 'Mrs Wakefield would never let anyone do that. Currant's secret is safe.'

Twilight nuzzled the mare. 'Lauren's right. No one at Orchard Stables would ever do anything to hurt Currant. You won't know whether Currant's a unicorn until he's a year old, when a

Unicorn Elder will visit him. Until then you can treat him like a normal foal.'

Apple snorted in relief.

'Is she going to be OK with people handling Currant now?' Lauren asked.

Apple whinnied.

'Yes,' Twilight interpreted. 'In fact, she says you can stroke him now if you like.'

Feeling very honoured, Lauren stepped forwards. She rubbed Currant's fluffy neck and he twisted his head round to nibble her sleeve.

'Hey!' she said, gently pushing his muzzle away. 'No biting, silly!'

Currant looked at her mischievously and blinked his long eyelashes.

Lauren giggled and stroked Currant's

soft nose. 'I hope you *are* a unicorn,' she murmured. 'Perhaps Grace will be your unicorn friend. She would be perfect and it would be brilliant to be able to share the secret with her. But I suppose we'll just have to wait to find out.'

Currant stepped away and butted his head underneath Apple's belly. Apple nuzzled his hindquarters with a contented sigh.

Lauren smiled. It was a very peaceful scene. 'Come on, let's leave them,' she whispered to Twilight.

They crept out of the stable. It was very dark now. As the stars shone down, Lauren gave Twilight a hug. 'I'm glad we've been able to help calm Apple.'

'So am I.' He rubbed his head against
her. 'And I'm glad we helped Jade, too.
You were amazing.'

'I couldn't have done it without you,'
Lauren told him. 'You made me believe I
could calm Apple down. I don't think
I could have gone into the stable if you
hadn't been there.'

'And I couldn't have got her out of

the stable on my own.' Twilight pushed her with his nose. 'I guess that's why unicorns have unicorn friends – you can do things that I can't and I can do things that you can't. We help each other help other people.'

Lauren realized he was right. Whatever problems they were facing – from rescuing Jade from the stable to cheering Buddy up – they solved the problems they faced together. She stroked his mane. 'We're a team, aren't we?'

Twilight nodded. 'We are.' He blew softly on her hair. 'I like us being a team, Lauren.'

Feeling very happy, Lauren put her arms around him. 'Me too,' she smiled.

My Secret Unicorn
Friends Forever

Lauren looked round to where the other Owls
had been but Jasmine, Natasha, Julia and Rose
had already left to go to the woods. Lauren
wondered if she should catch up with them.
But what would she say? Looking around,
she felt suddenly very alone.

She ran down to the paddocks. Hearing her
coming, Twilight whinnied in greeting and trotted
over to the gate. Lauren put her arms around
him. 'Oh, Twilight,' she whispered . . . 'I never
thought camp was going to be like this!'

To the real Jasmine, Rose and Natasha

CHAPTER
One

'Are you ready, Twilight?' Lauren whispered.

Twilight nodded. 'Yes.' He touched his glittering silver horn to the rock of rose quartz on the ground before them. 'Cedar Creek Riding Camp!' he declared.

A purple mist swirled over the rock and its pinky-grey surface began to shine like a mirror. As the smoke cleared,

Lauren saw a picture appearing. It showed a large grassy campsite with a horse barn, paddocks, three white cabins with window boxes full of flowers and a long low central building. Dark woods fringed the fields. Through them, Lauren could see the silvery gleam of a creek in the moonlight.

'Oh, wow!' Lauren breathed as she looked at Cedar Creek Camp. She was stroking Twilight's neck in delight. Most of the time, Twilight looked just like any other ordinary grey pony, but when Lauren said the words of the Turning Spell he changed into a beautiful white unicorn who could talk, do magic and fly. One of his magic powers meant that

when he touched his horn to a rock of
rose quartz he could see anything he
wanted, anywhere in the world.

'That's where we'll be tomorrow
night,' Twilight said, gazing into the rock.

Lauren nodded. She and Twilight were
going to the camp for six days. Mel,
Lauren's best friend, was going too, with
her pony, Shadow. 'It's going to be so
cool,' Lauren told Twilight happily. 'We
get to showjump and do cross-country
and go for rides in the woods and
there's all the other stuff like camp fires
and swimming in the creek.'

'I'm really looking forward to meeting
the other ponies,' Twilight said.

'Yeah,' agreed Lauren. 'And all the

new people. I wonder who Mel and I will be sharing our cabin with.'

'Only a few hours till we find out,' Twilight said excitedly.

Reluctantly, Lauren pulled her eyes away from the image in front of her. 'I think we should go home now. We're going to have to be up early in the morning.'

Twilight nodded. As he took his horn away from the rock, the picture faded. Lauren climbed on to his warm back. Cantering forward, Twilight plunged into the sky. As they swooped through the trees, Lauren's long fair hair whipped back from her face. Excitement buzzed through her as she thought about the next day. What was riding camp going to be like? She couldn't wait to find out!

'Look, girls!' Mrs Cassidy, Mel's mum, said the next day as, they drove towards a large white sign saying:

CEDAR CREEK CAMP THIS WAY!

'Hurray!' Mel cried. 'We're here!'

Mrs Cassidy turned in to a bumpy track that led into the woods.

'I wish Jess was with us,' Lauren said to Mel.

'We'll tell her all about it,' Mel replied. Jessica was their other best friend. She hadn't been able to come to

camp because she was going on holiday with her family.

Lauren nodded and then caught sight of water glinting through the trees. 'Look!'

'I wonder if that's Cedar Creek,' Mel said. 'You know, the creek that gave Cedar Creek Camp its name.'

'It is,' Lauren replied, remembering the magic images she'd seen the night before. 'It runs all the way through the woods up to the campsite.' She saw Mel look at her in surprise, and hastily added, 'I . . . I saw it on the map on the website.'

Mel grinned. 'I've been looking at the website a lot too. Last night, I was looking at the photos. I kept imagining being here.'

Phew, Lauren thought. Sometimes it was very hard to remember to keep Twilight's magic a secret from her family and friends!

The car and trailer bumped along the uneven track until they reached an open wooden gate. As Mrs Cassidy drove through it, Lauren could see Cedar Creek Riding Camp spread out before them. It looked just like it had when she and Twilight had seen it the night before, only it wasn't quiet and deserted any more: there were people and ponies everywhere!

Mrs Cassidy found a space near the barn and stopped the car. Lauren and Mel had the doors open before she'd even switched off the engine. Girls and their parents were unloading ponies from trailers all around them and lugging great heavy trunks and armfuls of tack across the field towards the barn.

'Look, that's where we'll be sleeping,' Mel said, pointing to the three white cabins nearby. They each had a small porch and cheerful window boxes, spilling over with pink and purple flowers.

'I wonder which cabin we'll be in,' Lauren said, watching a couple of girls carrying rucksacks into the middle cabin.

Just then, a woman bustled up to them. She was wearing navy jodhpurs

and a smart white polo shirt with the
Cedar Creek logo – a black horse
trotting through cedar trees – on the
front. Her shoulder-length brown hair,
slightly streaked with grey, was tucked
behind her ears and she was holding a
clipboard.

'Hello,' she said, smiling. 'And who
might you two be?'

'Lauren Foster and Mel Cassidy,'
replied Lauren.

'Pleased to meet you,' the woman
said, ticking their names off on her list.
'I'm Hilary. I own Cedar Creek and I'm
the senior instructor and counsellor. I
hope you'll have a great stay with us.'

Lauren thought she was going to like

Hilary. She had a no-nonsense air about her, but her smile was friendly.

As Mrs Cassidy came over to introduce herself, Lauren and Mel looked around.

'I wonder what we do now,' Mel said to Lauren.

Hilary overheard. 'First you need to get your ponies settled into their stalls.' She checked her list. 'Twilight and Shadow, isn't it?'

Mel and Lauren nodded.

'They're next door to each other in stalls seven and eight in the barn,' Hilary went on. 'When you've got them sorted you can start moving into your cabins.' She checked her clipboard again.

'Lauren, you'll be in the Owls cabin, which is the furthest on the right. Mel, you'll be in the Bluejays cabin, which is next door.'

Lauren blinked. For a moment, she wondered if she'd heard properly.

Next door!

'But we can't be in different cabins!' Mel exclaimed.

'We wanted to be in the same cabin!' Lauren protested. She and Mel had been planning on spending every moment at camp together.

Hilary looked at them sympathetically. 'Sorry, girls, but we have a policy here at Cedar Creek that campers should share with people they haven't arrived with.

We find it makes everyone mix much better. After all, part of the fun in coming to camp is meeting new people.' She smiled cheerfully. 'OK, I'll leave you to get sorted out. See you later.'

As she strode off, Lauren and Mel looked at each other in dismay.

CHAPTER
Two

Mel turned to Mrs Cassidy. 'Mum! Lauren and I have *got* to share a cabin!'

'Don't make a fuss, Mel,' Mrs Cassidy said. 'You heard what Hilary said and she's right. It will be a good way for you to make new friends.'

Mel's eyes filled with tears. 'But, Mum, we really want to be together. It won't be nearly so much fun if we're in different cabins. Please talk to Hilary. Please!'

'I'm sorry, Mel,' Mrs Cassidy replied, 'but it's obviously a camp rule.'

Lauren swallowed. 'I suppose it won't be that bad, Mel,' she said, feeling upset but trying very hard to make the best of it. 'After all, it's only for sleeping. We'll be with each other the rest of the time.'

Mel didn't look convinced.

Shadow whinnied impatiently from inside the trailer.

'I think Shadow's trying to tell us something,' Mrs Cassidy said. 'Come on, you two, stop looking so miserable and let's get those ponies out!'

★

Lauren and Mel settled Twilight and
Shadow into the barn. It had a wide
central aisle with nine stalls on either
side. At the far end was a large tack
room. Ponies were being put into stalls
and people were unloading their tack.
The air was full of excited chatter and
girls calling out to each other.

'Erin! Hi! Come and see my new pony!'

'Paige! You've had your hair cut!'

'Hey, Natasha, do you think we'll go riding bareback again this year?'

Lauren led Twilight into his stall. The excitement she'd felt when they had first arrived had fizzled out. She couldn't believe she and Mel were going to be in different cabins. They'd planned on having midnight feasts and telling ghost stories every night. Now they wouldn't be able to do any of those things. As she began to take off the travelling wraps that had protected Twilight's legs on the journey, she told him all about it.

'I really wish we were in the same cabin,' she finished sadly.

Twilight nuzzled her sympathetically.

Lauren gave him a hug. 'I'll come and talk to you later,' she said. 'I'd better go and unpack my things now.'

She and Mel headed back across the busy campsite to the car.

'Goodbye, girls,' Mrs Cassidy said as they heaved their rucksacks out of the car. 'Have a great time. I'll see you on Friday.'

They waved her off, then began to lug their rucksacks across the grass. All around them, other girls were saying goodbye to their parents too and heading towards the cabins. As they got closer to the three cabins, Mel's steps got slower.

'Come on,' Lauren said reassuringly. 'It's not going to be that bad.' Looking at her cabin, she hoped she was right!

As she pushed open the door, she saw that the cabin had three bunk beds and one single bed. Each bunk had a name label on the end of it. There was a stripy red rug on the floor and bright gingham curtains at the window. Four girls, all about Lauren's age, were sitting on one of the bottom bunks. They were all laughing together, but they broke off as Lauren came in.

'Hi,' Lauren said, feeling awkward as they all looked at her.

A small skinny girl with short fair

hair stood up. 'Hello,' she said. 'I'm Natasha. Are you Lauren?'

'Yes,' Lauren replied, relieved to see that Natasha smiled at her in a friendly way.

'We were wondering when you'd get here,' a girl with shoulder-length dark blonde hair said. 'We saw your name on your bunk bed. I'm Rose and this is Julia.' She tilted her head towards a girl with a long red plait.

'Hi,' Julia said shyly. Her voice was hardly louder than a whisper and she blushed as if embarrassed to be speaking out loud. 'I'm sharing this bunk with Rose.'

'And I'm sharing the bunk by the window with Natasha,' said the girl

sitting on the other side of Julia. She
bounced up. She was tall and slim with
wavy brown hair and sensible brown
eyes. 'My name's Jasmine. Is this your
first time at Cedar Creek, Lauren?'

Lauren nodded.

'Mine too,' Jasmine grinned. 'But it
seems cool. I don't have a pony of my
own,' she went on. 'I'm borrowing one

called Nugget from Hilary for the week. Mum and Dad say that they might buy me my own pony if I get on OK here.'

'I came here last year,' Natasha explained to Lauren. 'Julia was here then too. It was great!'

Julia nodded. 'Hilary and the other instructors are really nice,' she said quietly.

That's your bed over there, Lauren.' Natasha pointed to a bunk bed in the corner.

'Thanks,' Lauren replied. She walked over to it and looked eagerly to see the name of the person she'd be sharing it with. But there was only a single label saying *Lauren Foster* on the bed.

Jasmine saw her looking at the label.

'There's no one sharing with you,' she explained. 'Hope — she's the counsellor for this cabin — told us that a girl called Ellen was supposed to be staying in here with us but she got chickenpox and hasn't been able to come.'

'Oh,' Lauren said, feeling disappointed that she didn't have anyone to share with. She looked at the single bed in the opposite corner. 'Is that Hope's bed, then?'

'Yes,' Natasha replied. 'She's gone to check on her horse. She said he's got a sore foot.'

'She told us to unpack,' Jasmine put in. 'I think we should get a move on. She'll be back soon.'

Natasha nodded. 'You have to finish telling us about the show, Rose.'

Jasmine and Julia giggled, remembering what they'd been talking about when Lauren arrived.

'I can't believe you fell off twice,' Jasmine said, opening her rucksack.

Rose grinned. 'I told you. I was useless! There I was sitting in the saddle and it was like, *where's his head?*' She and the others started to laugh.

'What happened?' Lauren asked, keen to join in.

Rose shook her head. 'Oh, nothing important. It's just a silly story I was telling the others about the first show I took my pony Sinbad to.'

'Very silly,' Jasmine giggled.

Natasha began to pull things out of her rucksack. 'Falling off over his tail!' she grinned, glancing at Rose. 'Even *I've* never done that.'

Unable to join in, Lauren went over to her bunk bed and put her rucksack down. The others gradually stopped giggling and began to unpack too. Jasmine was asking Natasha about camp and Rose was talking quietly to Julia as they finished putting their things away in the small cupboards beside their bunks. Wishing she had someone to share her bunk with and talk to, Lauren glanced at the empty bunk above her. *If only Mel was here*, she thought longingly.

She thought about the next-door cabin. What was Mel doing? Was she thinking about her too?

The door opened and a girl of about eighteen came in. Her brown hair was pulled back from her cheerful face in a stubby ponytail. Seeing Lauren, she smiled. 'Hi, you must be Lauren Foster. I'm Hope, the counsellor for this cabin.'

'Hi,' Lauren said.

'If you need anything at all, just ask me,' Hope told her cheerfully. 'Now, you lot, are you all just about ready?' she asked, looking around. 'Hilary wants everyone to come to the recreation room before dinner for the welcome meeting.'

After putting the last of their things

away, the Owls followed Hope to the long, low building in the centre of the camp. One side was the dining-hall and the other was the recreation room where the campers could go during free time. There were old brown sofas in it, a ping-pong table at one end of the room, a TV and a craft table.

The other campers and counsellors were all there. Lauren saw Mel sitting on a sofa with five other girls. *They must be the Bluejays*, Lauren thought.

She wanted to go and sit with Mel but there wasn't any room on that sofa, so she went with her cabin and sat down on the sofa opposite. Mel looked much happier than she had when Lauren had

left her at the Bluejays door. A girl with
red shoulder-length curls was sitting next
to her. She had dancing green eyes and a
mischievous smile. Glancing across the
room, the red-headed girl whispered
something to Mel. Lauren saw Mel
giggle at her and grin.

Lauren felt a flicker of jealousy but
she squashed it down and tried to feel
pleased that Mel was making friends.
She wondered if the red-headed girl
and Mel were bunkmates.

Just then, Hilary clapped her hands.
'OK, guys, listen up! I won't keep you
for long – I imagine you're probably
starving – but I just want to introduce
everyone, give out the schedules and run

through some camp rules. First of all,
the introductions. As you all know, I'm
Hilary, the senior instructor. Your other
two instructors will be Tom, who's my
son –' she pointed to a young man who
looked about twenty – 'and Emily, who
is a graduate of the camp and is training
to be a riding instructor. Then there are
your cabin counsellors – Hope, Andrea
and Meagan – and our wonderful cook,
Karen.' A large lady wearing a white
apron smiled round at them. 'Any
problems, come and find any of us. Now,
on to the schedules,' Hilary started to
give out some sheets of paper. 'At Cedar
Creek we ride every morning, and then
we have an unmounted session after

lunch where we do things without the ponies — demonstrations and lessons on stable management, things like that. Then we have a fun riding session in the afternoon. We expect you to be up by seven-thirty to help with mucking out and grooming, breakfast is at nine and lessons start at ten after you've done your camp chores.'

The red-headed girl who'd been giggling with Mel stuck up her hand. 'What are camp chores?'

'Well, Kate, every day each cabin is given a chore to do — either sweeping the yard or cleaning up the tack room or something like that,' Hilary explained. She smiled. 'I know it might sound like a lot of work but don't worry. We just like you all to have some responsibility for keeping the camp neat and tidy. It's also part of the team competition.'

'Competition?' asked Jasmine.

'Yes, we have a competition for the best cabin. All week you have the chance to earn points in your cabin teams,' Hilary replied. 'You can get points in mounted competitions, for doing your chores, for keeping your cabins tidy and for the turnout of you and your pony at the start of each day. At the end of the week the team with the most points will win a trophy each.'

Lauren glanced at Mel. The competition sounded fun but it would have been even better if she and Mel had been in the same team.

'And just so you know,' Hilary went on, 'your free time is your own, but we do ask that campers don't go into each other's cabins after dinner and, from that time in the evening, the stables are also out of bounds.

'Out of bounds!' The words burst out of Lauren before she could stop them.

Hilary nodded. 'Yes, we've found that ponies don't appreciate late-night gossip and midnight feasts as much as their riders!' She looked round at them all. 'It's my guess that you lot would be in the barn all night if you were allowed to, but the ponies really do need time to

sleep and relax, so no going into the
barn after dinner, OK?'

The other campers nodded but Lauren
was too stunned to respond. Her thoughts
were reeling. If the barn was out of
bounds then she couldn't go and see
Twilight at night; that meant no talking –
and no flying – for a whole week!

CHAPTER
Three

When Hilary had finished her talk, the campers headed into the dining-hall for dinner. Lauren followed the other Owls, but her mind was on Twilight. She'd never imagined that the stables would be out of bounds. *Maybe no one will notice if I sneak out there*, she thought hopefully.

The dining-hall was laid out with five

tables covered with cheerful checked
tablecloths. Along one side there was a
counter set out with an enormous dish
of macaroni cheese, huge platters of hot
dogs and a salad bar. Everyone crowded
around the food table, laughing and
talking. Lauren helped herself and then
went looking for Mel.

She found her sitting at a table by the
window with three of the other
Bluejays. There was still some space at
the table and Lauren headed over. The
Bluejays were flicking bread at each
other with their fingers.

'Got you, Erin!' Kate shouted as a piece
of bread bounced off the spiky-haired
girl's nose.

Erin grinned and flicked a piece back.
It missed and flew over Kate's shoulder,
landing on the Eagles' table. They looked
round mystified and the Bluejays burst
out laughing.

'Hi!' Lauren said, raising her voice to
speak above the scraping of chairs on
the floor and the noisy chattering of the
dining-hall.

Kate looked her up and down. 'Who
are you?' she said in a not-altogether
friendly way.

'This is Lauren, my best friend from
home,' Mel said. 'Lauren, this is Kate –
who I'm sharing a bunk with, Erin
and Paige,' she added nodding to a
quieter girl with a blonde ponytail

and the girl with the spiky hair.

Paige smiled but Kate and Erin didn't.

'Sit down, Lauren,' urged Mel.

But before Lauren could, a girl came
over from the serving area.

'Hey, Allison, come and sit with us!'
Kate called, pointing to the seat beside
Mel.

'Thanks,' said the girl as she sat down. She grinned. 'So we've got ourselves a Bluejays table.'

Mel looked as if she didn't know what to do. Lauren gave a shrug. 'It's OK,' she said quietly to Mel. 'I should probably go and sit with the rest of my cabin.' She tried to sound like she didn't care, but she did — she cared a lot. She hoped Mel would offer to come with her but she didn't.

Feeling a bit hurt, Lauren went over to where the Owls were sitting. As she sat down, she glanced round. Mel was trying to take an enormous bite of her hot dog and giggling as Kate tickled her at the same time. Lauren looked at

her meal. Suddenly she didn't feel quite
so hungry any more.

All through dinner, Lauren heard giggles
coming from the Bluejays' table and soon
bits of bread were flying round the
room, until Emily noticed and told them
to clear it all up. Lauren tried to be glad
that Mel was getting on so well with her
cabinmates, but it was hard. *She* wanted
to be having fun with Mel. Next to her,
Julia was busy talking to Natasha and
across the table, Jasmine was talking to
Rose. Lauren suppressed a sigh and ate
in silence.

After dinner was over and the plates
had been cleared away, the Bluejays went

through to the recreation room and
started playing a noisy game of snap. It
looked like fun. *I suppose I could always
go and ask if I could play too*, Lauren
thought as she went into the room.

'Hi,' Mel greeted her as she walked
over.

'Snap! I won!' Erin shouted, scooping
up all the cards. 'New game!'

'Can I play?' Lauren asked.

Kate jumped to her feet. 'Sorry, but
we're done playing now. We're going
back to the cabin – we need to talk
tactics for the team cup. We are *so* going
to win it!'

The others grinned and began to
stand up too.

Lauren looked at Mel. 'Are you going too?'

Mel looked awkward. 'Um –'

'What are you waiting for, Mel?' Kate interrupted her. 'See you tomorrow, Lisa.'

'Lauren,' Lauren corrected her. 'My name's Lauren.'

Kate shrugged as if it didn't matter. 'Come on, Mel.'

Mel got to her feet. 'I'll see you tomorrow, OK?' she said to Lauren.

Lauren nodded. Her throat felt tight.

Mel went off with the others.

A great wave of homesickness suddenly swept over Lauren and, biting her lip, she hurried out of the door.

She ran across the grass towards her cabin. The barn loomed in the distance. As she looked at it, she suddenly wanted to talk to Twilight. *No one will notice*, she thought. *They're all busy.* Changing direction she ran towards the barn.

She reached it without anyone seeing her and opened the doors just enough to slip inside. Hay nets were hanging outside the stalls for the morning and there was no sound apart from the occasional snort and stamp of a hoof.

'Twilight!' Lauren whispered.

From his stall near the tack room, Twilight gave a welcoming snicker.

Lauren ran down the aisle and slid the bolts on his door across. Stepping into the warm stall, she put her arms around his smooth neck. 'Oh, Twilight, I'm glad to see you,' she told him. 'I'm feeling really lonely and I badly wanted to talk to you. But I can't stay long. I'm not supposed to be here.' She said the words of the Turning Spell.

> '*Twilight Star, Twilight Star,*
> *Twinkling high above so far.*
> *Shining light, shining bright,*
> *Will you grant my wish tonight?*
> *Let my little horse forlorn*
> *Be at last a unicorn!*'

A bright purple flash lit up the dark barn and Twilight turned into a unicorn. His grey coat suddenly gleamed snow-white and his mane and tail shone silver.

'What do you mean, you're not supposed to be here?' he asked in surprise.

Lauren explained about the camp rule. 'The barn is out of bounds after dinner, which means I'm not going to be able

to come here at night unless I sneak out, and just hope no one sees me.'

'That sounds a bit risky.' Twilight looked worried.

Lauren nodded. 'I don't know what to do. It'll be really weird not turning you into a unicorn all week.'

'No magic for a whole week,' Twilight said slowly.

They stared at each other.

'I suppose there'll be lots of other things to do,' Lauren said, stroking him.

Twilight nodded. 'You shouldn't risk it. If you get caught here, you'll get in trouble and . . .'

Suddenly he stiffened and broke off. 'Lauren, I think I just heard something outside!' He looked towards the door. His horn started to glow as he used his magic powers to make his hearing extra-sensitive. 'Yes! There's definitely someone coming!'

Lauren gabbled out the words of the Undoing Spell and, in an instant, Twilight changed back. Lauren ran out of the stall cursing herself for leaving the barn door open. Could she get out of the barn without being discovered?

The beam of a torch swung round the aisle.

She was too late.

'Who's there?' a voice asked sharply.

Lauren froze. It was Hilary!

CHAPTER
Four

The torch caught Lauren in its beam.

'What are you doing in here?' Hilary asked, coming down the aisle.

Lauren's cheeks felt like they were on fire. 'I . . . I just wanted to see Twilight,' she whispered, wishing she was somewhere – *anywhere* – else.

There was a moment's silence and

then Hilary sighed and her voice softened. 'It's your first time at camp, isn't it, Lauren? Were you feeling homesick?'

Lauren nodded.

'It happens to a lot of people on the first night. You'll soon settle in,' Hilary said gently. 'But you *must* obey the camp rules. We really can't have campers in the barn at night without adult supervision. Now, seeing as it's the first night, let's just forget I ever found you here. But,' she added warningly, 'it really mustn't happen again. If it does, I'm afraid I'll have no choice but to send you home. I can't have campers deliberately breaking the rules. Do you understand?'

'I understand,' Lauren replied.

Hilary smiled. 'Good girl. Say
goodnight to Twilight and run on back
to your cabin before the bedtime bell
goes.'

Lauren got back to the Owls' cabin

just as the bell began to ring. The others looked at her curiously.

'Where have you been?' Natasha asked.

'Just around,' Lauren said vaguely.

She went to the tiny bathroom, brushed her teeth and got changed into her pyjamas. It felt strange climbing into the unfamiliar bunk beds. As Hope said goodnight and turned off the light, she heard the creaks of the others shifting in their beds and the quiet sound of their breathing as they gradually fell asleep.

Lauren stared at the bed above her and thought about Mel next door. Was she having trouble sleeping too? This just wasn't how she'd imagined her first night at camp would be at all!

'Come on, guys, you've got to get them cleaner than that!' Kate's voice rang out across the grooming area the next morning, as she bossed the other Bluejays around. 'We want to get loads of points in the grooming inspection so that we can win the cup.'

Brushing out the tangles in Twilight's tail, Lauren frowned. They'd only been up an hour and already Kate was annoying her. While the Owls and the Eagles were grooming quietly, Kate was charging about, noisily organizing the Bluejays. Lauren had hardly had a chance to speak to Mel because Mel had been far too busy trying to get Shadow's coat clean enough to meet with Kate's approval.

Rose came up to Natasha, who was standing near Lauren. 'Kate's a bit bossy, isn't she?' she said in a low voice.

'You can say that again,' Natasha muttered back.

'She's acting like it's a show or something,' Rose said, watching as Kate carefully removed a remaining speck of dirt from her pony's coat with a damp cloth and then put some spray on his mane to make it lie perfectly flat. 'We're only having a lesson.'

But when the time came for Hilary,

Tom and Emily to inspect the ponies before the lesson, it became obvious that Kate's bossiness had paid off. The Bluejays' ponies looked spotlessly clean and the team marks reflected it.

'Eagles, we've given you six marks. Owls, you got seven and the Bluejays did exceptionally well, you get ten out of ten,' Hilary announced.

Kate whooped, causing several ponies to jump in alarm.

'And for the cabin inspection this morning,' Hilary went on checking her sheet. 'Bluejays get ten out of ten again, Eagles seven and Owls six.'

All the Bluejays cheered.

Hilary clapped her hands for

attention. 'OK, Owls you'll be with me
for a riding lesson. Bluejays and Eagles,
you'll be doing showjumping with Tom
and Emily.'

As the showjumping groups left the
arena to ride into the field, Lauren
gathered up her reins.

'Are you ready, everyone?' Hilary

called out to the Owls. 'Prepare to walk
. . . and walk on.'

Lauren and Twilight set off, and
Lauren hoped that the first riding lesson
would be more fun than the chores had
been.

Despite not being with Mel, Lauren
really enjoyed the lesson. She didn't have
riding lessons at home and Hilary was a
good teacher. She explained things
clearly and was quick to praise any
improvement in the campers' riding.
Lauren learnt how to leg yield, which
meant getting the pony to step sideways
but forward at the same time so they
moved diagonally across the ring. At first

she could only get Twilight to take a couple of steps but by the end of the lesson he was going all the way from the centre of the arena to the outside.

'Great work, Lauren,' Hilary praised her. 'I can see you're a fast learner!'

Lauren blushed but her heart leapt. She patted Twilight's neck. 'Good boy,' she said.

After the lesson, they put the ponies out in the fields. Twilight and Shadow were sharing a paddock with Rose's pony, Sinbad, and Nugget, the pony that Jasmine was borrowing for camp.

'Hi!' Mel called to Lauren as she led Shadow to the paddock. 'We had a great lesson!' she said excitedly. 'We did lots of jumping. How about you? Your lesson didn't look as much fun as ours.'

'Well, it was! It was really good!' Lauren knew she sounded crabby but she couldn't help feeling hurt that Mel had hardly said a single word to her that morning.

Mel shot her a surprised look. 'What's up with you?'

'Nothing,' Lauren sighed. 'Sorry, I didn't mean to snap. I'm just hungry.'

'Me too,' agreed Mel. 'Let's go and get some lunch.'

After putting the ponies out, they got changed into shorts and went to the dining-hall. There was a salad bar set up again and a make-your-own sandwich table. Lauren and Mel made a pile of peanut butter sandwiches and cream cheese and ham bagels, and then filled their trays up with crisps, apples and a huge glass each of chilled lemonade.

They went to sit outside together. As they talked about their lessons, Lauren felt the tension that had been building up inside her slowly fade away. This was how she'd imagined camp to be – she and Mel having a great time and talking about their favourite thing – horses!

'So what are the other Owls like?' Mel asked.

'OK,' Lauren replied. 'Pretty quiet.'

'The other Bluejays are *definitely* not

quiet!' Mel grinned. 'We had a huge pillow fight last night and tonight Kate wants us to tell ghost stories!'

Lauren felt a stab of jealousy. She and Mel had planned to tell ghost stories at night. But that was when they'd thought they'd be sharing a cabin.

'Kate's really good fun,' Mel enthused.

'She seems a bit bossy,' Lauren said shortly.

'A bit,' Mel said. 'But she's really cool *and* she's a brilliant rider.'

Lauren didn't want to spend lunchtime listening to Mel talking about how great Kate was. She quickly changed the subject. 'Shall we go to the creek when we've finished eating?'

Mel nodded. 'Yeah! We should have time before the unmounted session. What's your team doing this afternoon?'

'Getting a pony ready for a show,' Lauren replied. 'How about you?'

'We've got a talk on Western tack,' Mel replied.

Lauren sighed. 'I wish we were in the same team and we could go to things together.'

'I know,' Mel said, 'but at least everyone else is really fun.'

Everyone in your cabin, Lauren thought. It wasn't that she disliked the other Owls, but they didn't seem to have as much fun as the Bluejays.

Mel got to her feet. 'Come on, I'm

finished. Let's dump our plates and go to
the creek.'

Lauren jumped to her feet and
followed her across the grass.

Lauren and Mel had fun paddling in
the creek. There were seven other

campers there too, mainly from the Eagles' cabin, and Meagan and Emily were supervising.

When it was almost time for the afternoon sessions to start, Lauren and Mel headed back to the barn. As they reached it, Kate came running out from behind it, chasing Erin and Allison across the grass with a wet sponge in each hand. She chucked the sponges and they splattered against Erin and Allison's shorts. 'Yuck!' Allison exclaimed, chucking the sponge back. Kate ducked, laughing.

'Hey, Mel!' she shouted. 'Where have you been? We've been having a water fight. Now we're going to go to the hay barn before the Western thing. There's a rope hanging from the ceiling and you can swing on it. Want to come? We've got ten minutes before the demonstration.'

'Sure!' Mel replied. She turned to Lauren. 'Come on.'

Lauren hesitated. She wasn't sure Kate's invitation had included her.

'The Owls are all in the main barn if you're looking for them, Lauren,' Kate called out.

Guess I was right, Lauren thought. *She didn't want me to come!*

'Come on, Mel. You can see Lauren later,' Kate shouted.

Mel looked at Lauren. 'Um . . .'

Please Mel, don't go with them, Lauren thought.

'I'd better go with the others. See you later, Lauren,' Mel said, and she hurried off towards the other Bluejays. 'Wait for me, Kate! I'm coming!'

Lauren stood and stared. How *could* Mel have gone off like that? It was bad enough that they were separated in the evenings and for the lessons and demonstrations without Mel going off at other times too.

She watched as Mel ran into the hay barn with the other Bluejays.

'Thanks, Mel,' Lauren muttered. 'Thanks a lot!'

CHAPTER
Five

After the unmounted demonstrations,
everyone went on a trail ride.
Despite still feeling hurt about Mel going
off with Kate at lunchtime, Lauren
hoped they would finally get to ride
together. But some of the ponies weren't
used to being in the woods so Hilary
explained that she wanted to team the
nervous ponies with the steady ones.

'Lauren, Twilight seems very calm. Would you mind riding with Rose, please?' Hilary said as she organized everyone into pairs. 'Sinbad isn't used to being in the woods, is he, Rose?'

'No,' Rose replied, 'he gets a bit nervous riding through trees.'

'Well, I'm sure Twilight will help steady him,' Hilary said. 'He seems a very sensible sort of pony.'

She smiled at Lauren. Lauren forced a smile. back.

When everyone was sorted into pairs, the ride set off. There were a lot of them but it was fun trotting and cantering through the woods together.

At first Sinbad – Rose's young dapple-grey pony – was nervous, looking round at everything with wide eyes and shying at tree stumps and branches that cracked underfoot on the sandy trails. But Twilight kept touching him with his nose in a reassuring way and gradually Sinbad started to relax.

'He really likes Twilight,' Rose said to Lauren when they slowed to a walk.

Lauren smiled at her. She liked Rose. 'How long have you had Sinbad?'

'Two years. How about you and Twilight?'

'Just one year,' Lauren replied.

She was about to ask Rose more about Sinbad when Hilary gave the instruction to trot on again, and they had to concentrate on their riding. They were out for almost two hours in the shade of the trees. Afterwards they cooled the ponies down in the creek and then turned them out in the paddocks. Then they set to work cleaning their tack.

Mel went and sat with the other Bluejays right away. Lauren hesitated and took her tack over to where the Owls were sitting.

I'll talk to her when we finish, Lauren thought, glancing across at her best friend. *We can do something together before dinner.*

'Are you OK?'

Lauren looked round. It was Jasmine who'd spoken.

'Umm . . . yes,' Lauren replied.

'It's just you seem quiet,' Jasmine said. She looked in the direction of the Bluejays. 'Is it because your friend Mel is over there?'

Lauren nodded.

'It must be weird – having your best
friend here and not being in the same
cabin,' Jasmine said sympathetically. She
looked at the others. 'Look, why don't
we all go into the woods when we've
finished and practise for this quiz.'
Lauren remembered that there was going
to be a team pony quiz after dinner that
night. 'There are some tree stumps we
can sit on and we can take some stable
management books with us,' Jasmine
went on.

'OK,' Rose agreed. Natasha and Julia
nodded.

Lauren hesitated. She wanted to go
but if she did, she wouldn't be able to
see Mel. 'Thanks but I don't think I

will,' she told them. She saw their looks
of surprise. 'I was going to meet up
with Mel,' she said by way of an excuse.

Jasmine shrugged. 'OK.' She turned
back to cleaning her bridle and didn't
say anything more.

Lauren felt bad. She knew Jasmine had just been trying to be friendly. She finished her tack and then went over to the Bluejays. They looked up as she approached. Lauren felt awkward. 'Um, hi, Mel,' she said, feeling very aware they were all listening. 'When . . . when you've finished your tack, do you want to come back to my cabin? I thought we could look at some books before this quiz tonight.'

Mel frowned. 'Um, that would be good but –'

'She can't,' Kate interrupted. 'Sorry, but we're having a team meeting. *Just* for the Bluejays,' she added.

'Oh.' Lauren glanced at Mel.

Mel shrugged awkwardly. 'Sorry, Lauren. I'll see you later, OK?'

Lauren swallowed. 'Yep,' she muttered. 'OK.'

Feeling her eyes suddenly start to fill, she swung round. She wasn't going to cry in front of them. She wasn't!

She looked round to where the other Owls had been but Jasmine, Natasha, Julia and Rose had already left to go to the woods. Lauren wondered if she should catch up with them. But what would she say? Looking around, she felt suddenly very alone.

She ran down to the paddocks. Hearing her coming, Twilight whinnied in greeting and trotted over to the gate.

Lauren put her arms around him. 'Oh, Twilight,' she whispered, her heart feeling like a lead weight in her chest. 'I never thought camp was going to be like this!'

Although Lauren was feeling low, the pony quiz that evening turned out to be much more fun than she had expected. She had always found it easy to remember pony things, and Natasha, Rose, Jasmine and Julia knew a lot too. Hilary called out questions. The person who got the answer right first won their team a chance to answer three more questions and get more points. The Owls' hands were the first up for nearly

every question. Lauren got so involved
in it that she forgot to think about Mel
at all. It was really good fun coming
up with the answers for the team
questions with the other Owls, especially
since they got so many answers right!
They won the quiz easily and were
given a bag of sweets to share and six
points towards their team-cup total.

'That was brilliant!' Rose exclaimed as
they shared the sweets out. 'I can't
believe we did so well.'

'You answered loads of questions,
Lauren,' Jasmine put in.

'And you didn't even practise with us,'
Natasha said.

Lauren thought about two questions

she'd got wrong and felt slightly guilty. 'I should have done,' she said, meaning it. 'Then I might not have messed up those two questions.'

'It wouldn't have made any difference,' Rose told her. 'And you got more starter questions right than the rest of us.'

Lauren grinned at her happily.

'We're only one point behind the Bluejays now!' Natasha exclaimed. 'We *must* do well in the pony inspection tomorrow.'

They all agreed, and going to bed that night Lauren realized that she felt happier than she had done all camp. She set her alarm clock for six-thirty.

Twilight was going to look spotless the next morning!

When Lauren's alarm clock rang, she jumped out of bed. She and the others went to the barn and set to work washing tails and grooming until their ponies shone. Kate looked very surprised to see them all there when she and the rest of the Bluejays came to the barn at seven o'clock. She scowled when she saw how clean the Owls' ponies were looking. Lauren hid a grin. The Owls were going to get as many points as the Bluejays that morning, she was sure of it!

After breakfast, they got changed into

their riding clothes and then went back to tack up.

As Lauren finished doing up Twilight's girth, she stood back to admire him. But as she did so, her foot bumped into a bucket of dirty water that had been put down just behind her. It overturned with a clatter and splashed everywhere, dirty droplets of water splattering Lauren's cream jodhpurs and soaking Twilight's front legs.

Lauren gasped in horror.

'Oh, Lauren!' Rose exclaimed. 'Why didn't you clear that bucket away?'

'I didn't leave it there!' Lauren said.

Hearing a snort of laughter, she swung round. Kate and Erin were giggling. 'What a pity. You won't get full marks for your turnout now,' Kate said.

Lauren shot her a furious look. 'Did you put that bucket there?'

'No,' Kate said quickly. But her eyes danced mischievously.

Lauren glanced at Mel but she was talking to Paige at the other end of the horse line and hadn't noticed.

'Quick, Lauren!' Jasmine urged. 'You'd better get on. Hilary, Tom and Emily are coming!'

Lauren brushed away the water as best she could and mounted. After all her hard work, it wasn't fair! Now her team would lose points. She just knew Kate had put the bucket there.

To her relief, Hilary only knocked two points off their total. 'I can see it must have been an accident,' she said. 'The rest of Twilight is beautifully groomed, Lauren.'

Kate looked disappointed.

'So that's ten out of ten for the Bluejays, eight for the Owls and six for the Eagles,' Hilary announced, checking her clipboard. 'If you can get into your rides, please. Eagles with me, Owls with Tom and Bluejays with Emily.'

The jumping lesson was really fun. Tom put out a line of low jumps. All five ponies jumped very well, so Tom made the girls take their stirrups away.

'Well done,' he said as they completed the jumps. 'Let's try jumping a bit higher now.'

He dragged a jump to the centre of the field and raised the bar.

'That looks big,' Jasmine said nervously.

'Who'll go first?' Tom asked.

'I will,' Lauren offered.

Twilight jumped the new fence easily, as did all the other ponies apart from Nugget. The first time he jumped it OK, but after that he started refusing. Jasmine looked anxious, and she was sitting stiffly in the saddle. 'You have to relax,' Tom told her. 'Nugget can jump it easily.'

Jasmine got Nugget over the jump one more time, but as he landed he threw up his head and after that he refused the fence every single time. She began to look very frustrated. Tom walked over to help her. 'Get off and give your ponies a rest for a few minutes,' he told the others.

As Lauren dismounted, she looked across to the other end of the jumping field where the Bluejays were jumping a bright-red wall with pots of white flowers beside it. Lauren wondered how Shadow would cope. Until recently he had been very scared of jumping. Lauren and Twilight had visited him at night and helped him overcome his fear. But

he still didn't like jumping unusual
fences. Lauren led Twilight over to
watch.

Shadow refused the wall the first time
he reached it.

'He hasn't jumped a wall like this before,' Mel explained to Emily.

'Why don't you take him up to it, Mel?' Kate called out from where she was sitting on her black pony, Chess. 'Circle it a few times so he can have a good look.'

'Thank you, Kate,' Emily commented dryly. 'I'm quite capable of taking the lesson.'

Kate grinned at her. 'Sorry, Em!'

'Still, what you said was good advice,' Emily agreed. 'Mel, why don't you do what Kate suggested?'

Mel let Shadow have a good look at the wall and then circled round it. When he was cantering smoothly and calmly she turned towards it. He flew over it easily.

'Good boy!' Mel exclaimed. She rode back to the line. Kate grinned at her and leant over Chess's neck. She seemed to be giving Mel more advice. Mel nodded eagerly.

Lauren's stomach clenched. She was the one Mel usually turned to for advice! She quickly turned Twilight away.

'Hi, Lauren,' Mel said, catching up with her after the lesson. 'Want to go and get some lunch?'

Lauren nodded briefly. She was in a bad mood. She couldn't stop thinking

about the way Mel had listened so
eagerly to Kate during the lesson.

As they headed to the dining–hall,
Mel sighed happily. 'We had a really
good lesson. Kate gave me some really
useful tips for jumping Shadow. She just
knew exactly what to do. She's brilliant!'

Hurt surged through Lauren. Mel
knew nothing about the many nights
she and Twilight had visited Shadow's
field when he was still scared of
jumping. If it hadn't been for her and
Twilight, Shadow would still have been
refusing to jump anything at all!

'I'm going to ask her if she'll help me
when we do cross-country jumping
tomorrow,' Mel went on happily. 'She'll

know what I should do. She's such a
good rider.'

'She's not that good!' Lauren snapped,
feeling totally fed up.

Mel looked at her in surprise. 'She *is*
good and she knows loads.'

Lauren's hurt boiled over. 'Yeah,
including how to steal people's best
friends!' She glared at Mel. 'Seeing as
you like Kate so much, why don't you
go and have lunch with *her*? It's not like
I matter, is it?'

Leaving Mel standing open-mouthed,
Lauren marched away.

CHAPTER

Six

So much for Mel and me being best friends, Lauren raged inwardly as she ran across the camp to the pony fields.

But gradually her fury started to fade. She hated arguments and she hated falling out with Mel most of all.

Twilight was standing with Nugget in the paddock. The two ponies were using their teeth to groom the other's withers.

Shadow was grazing a little way off, his nose almost touching Sinbad's as they pulled at the short grass. They all looked very happy.

It's OK for ponies, Lauren thought miserably. *They just get on with each other.*

Twilight came over to the fence and nudged her enquiringly.

'Oh, Twilight!' Lauren burst out. 'Mel keeps going off with Kate.' She quickly told him about the argument. 'I wish Kate wasn't here,' she finished despairingly. 'I wish it was just Mel and me.'

He nuzzled her hair and she hugged him, pressing her face against his neck and blinking back her tears.

'Lauren!'

Lauren jumped and swung round. Jasmine was walking towards her with Rose.

'Hi,' Rose started to say and then she saw Lauren's face. 'Hey, are you OK?' she asked in concern.

'Yes . . . no . . .' Lauren broke off and sniffed.

Jasmine put her hand on Lauren's arm. 'What's the matter?' she said.

Lauren bit her lip. 'I've had an argument with Mel.'

'Oh.' Jasmine looked like she didn't know what to say.

'A bad one?' Rose asked.

Lauren nodded.

'Well, we were about to go down to

the creek to swim with Hope. Do you
want to come too?' Rose asked, putting
a hand on her arm.

Lauren hesitated. What she really felt
like doing was going back to the cabin
and crying.

'Come on,' Jasmine urged. 'It'll be fun.'

Lauren looked from one to the other.
Their faces were friendly and concerned,
and as she looked at them, Lauren felt a

sudden wave of determination. Why should she be unhappy while Mel was having a great time with all her new friends? She could make new friends too! She remembered the quiz. It had been fun.

'OK,' she said, and she smiled. 'Thanks, I'd like that.'

'Let's go and find Julia and Natasha and see if they want to come too,' Rose said.

Lauren smiled. 'Sounds good to me!'

It didn't take them long to find Julia and Natasha. They got changed and hurried down to the creek where Hope and Emily were supervising some of the

Eagles as they played in the water. A tyre had been hung from a tree branch, and soon Lauren and the other Owls were taking it in turns to swing across the water from one bank to the other.

The sun shone down through the trees and the cold water glittered. Rose and Natasha had just managed to swing safely across.

'Come on, Julia! It's your turn!' Rose urged.

Julia looked at Lauren. 'No, one of you go first.'

'Go on, you'll be fine,' Lauren told her.

Julia took a deep breath and grinned nervously. 'Here goes!' Holding the rope she swung across. She fell just short, her feet landing in the water. She squealed and scrambled up the bank.

The rope came swinging back to Lauren. She grabbed it and took a breath. 'Come on, Lauren!' the others cried from the far bank, its sides slippery with mud.

Lauren swung out over the water but as she did so, she felt her hands start to slip. She tried to hang on, but it was too late, and her hands slipped down the rope. She tumbled into the water with a splash.

It wasn't deep but it was very cold. She surfaced, gasping. On the bank, the others were falling about, laughing so hard they could barely stand up.

Laughing too, Lauren started to splash great handfuls of water at them. Rose squealed and Natasha pushed her in. She slid down the slope and into the water. The splash drenched Julia who grabbed at Jasmine and Natasha. The next minute all three of them were sliding into the water too. Shrieking and giggling, they jumped around in the creek.

'That was fun!' Natasha said as they wrapped towels around themselves and sat in the sunlight to dry afterwards.

'It was awesome!' Lauren agreed, her eyes shining.

'Are you feeling happier now?' Jasmine asked her.

'Much,' Lauren replied. For a fleeting moment a picture of Mel crossed her mind but she pushed it away. Mel had her new friends. *I don't need her*, Lauren thought. 'We should do something tonight,' she said, remembering Mel's tales of pillow fights and ghost stories and midnight feasts in her cabin. 'How about we tell ghost stories?'

'Cool!' Natasha exclaimed.

'I don't like ghost stories,' Julia said.

'Oh, Julia!' the others groaned.

Julia hesitated. 'All right. We can tell ghost stories,' she agreed.

'Eight o'clock tonight,' Jasmine declared.

'Eight o'clock tonight,' they all echoed

and then everyone started talking about
the scariest ghost stories they knew.

Lauren sighed happily. There were
four days left at camp. She was going to
start having some fun!

Lauren hardly saw Mel for the next two
days. Every moment seemed to be full.

They had jumping and flat lessons, a dressage demonstration, a barbecue and a bareback ride. When they weren't taking part in organized activities she hung out with the other Owls in the cabin and at the barn. Although she had thought they were quite quiet, it turned out they weren't at all. The better Lauren got to know them, the more she realized how much fun they were. She could tell Kate was pleased that she and Mel had argued but she tried not to care. A couple of times during meals or when they were getting the ponies ready, Lauren caught Mel looking at her. She had a feeling Mel wanted to make up, but Lauren just couldn't bring herself to say sorry.

Mel shouldn't have gone off with Kate and the other Bluejays, she thought.

Yes, but you shouldn't have shouted at her like that, a sensible voice said in her head. Lauren ignored it.

The only downside of camp, now that she'd made new friends, was that she didn't get a chance to turn Twilight into a unicorn at all. She didn't dare go to the barn in the evenings, just in case Hilary caught her again. She didn't want to be sent home for breaking camp rules. She wanted to see Twilight and was missing talking to him, but she knew she couldn't risk it.

By the afternoon of the fourth day, the competition for the team cup was heating up. All three teams were within eight points of each other, and Hilary announced that there was going to be a mounted games competition that afternoon, with more points to be won towards the team totals.

The Bluejays had very fast ponies. They won the Sack Race, the Flag Race and were second in the Bending Race and in the Walk, Trot and Gallop. But the Owls also did well and by the last race, they were just ten points behind the Bluejays. The Eagles had fallen quite a long way behind.

The final race was called Groom, Get My Horse. The riders had to take it in turns to gallop to the top of the arena

and then they had to dismount, leave
their pony with a helper and run back.
As soon as they crossed the starting
line the next person in the team could
set off.

Lauren did a quick calculation. 'If we
can win this and the Bluejays come last,
we'll nearly make up the points
difference,' she said to the other girls.

Beside them, the Bluejays were
exchanging high-fives.

'They're not likely to come last,'
Jasmine commented.

The warning whistle went and
everyone got ready. At the front of the
Bluejays' line, Paige's pony, a very fast
but excitable Arab called Stella, was

tossing her head. Just as the whistle went the excitement got too much for her and she ran backwards. Jasmine, who was going first for the Owls, set off on Nugget like a bolt of lightning, leaving the other two teams way behind.

Lauren and the others cheered her on as she galloped to the top of the arena. Throwing her reins to Hope, she jumped off and began running back. She had enough of a lead to reach the Owls first. Natasha set off next, and then Julia. They were all fast runners but so were the Bluejays. By the time Rose jumped off, she and Allison were neck and neck. Lauren was waiting, her heart pounding as Rose started to run back.

Next to her, Kate was leaning forward, her eyes fixed on Allison. 'Come on, come on!' she was shouting.

Lauren's fingers curled in Twilight's mane. 'Please, boy,' she whispered, 'gallop as fast as you can!'

Rose came running back. Suddenly Kate was away. Lauren gasped. Allison hadn't got back to the starting line yet. That was cheating! But she didn't have time to think about it. Rose crossed the line and she was off. As Twilight galloped flat out to the end of the arena, Lauren was dimly aware of the sound of a whistle blowing and some commotion behind her, but she focused on riding to the fence. Hope was waiting. Lauren threw the reins at her. 'Good boy!' she gasped to Twilight as she flung herself off and turned to run. But the sight in front of her made her falter for a second. Kate had fallen off! She didn't look hurt but she certainly looked mad.

Suddenly Lauren was aware of Kirsty, a girl in the Eagles team, racing past her. She charged after her.

'Go, Lauren, go!' her team screamed.

Lauren caught up with Kirsty and passed her just as they reached the line. There was one more rider for each team still to go – Jasmine was riding a second time for the Owls since they only had five girls on their team. She and Jenny, who was the last person on the Eagles team, were very close, but Sara, who was the last Bluejay to ride, was quite a way behind them. Jasmine managed to pull just ahead of Jenny on the way back and crossed the finishing line first!

The Owls squealed with delight.

'We won! We won!' Natasha gasped.

'What happened to Kate?' Lauren panted, still trying to catch her breath after her turn. The race had all happened so quickly!

'Kate set off too early. Hilary saw and blew the whistle, so she had to turn a circle but Chess was really excited and he bucked and she fell off!' Julia gasped.

'Oh, Lauren. You should have seen her face!'

'She is OK, isn't she?' Lauren asked, her eyes flying to where Kate was brushing the dust from her jodhpurs.

'Yeah, she's fine,' Rose told her. 'But that means we're only four points behind them now! We might still be able to win the cup tomorrow.'

Lauren grinned with delight.

Hilary blew the whistle and called for order. Then she announced the points. Just as Lauren and her team had thought, they were only four points behind the Bluejays. The Eagles were fifteen points behind them.

'So, it's all going to be down to the last day,' Hilary said. 'Instead of having a lesson you'll be taking part in a team competition.'

'What's the competition going to be?' Natasha asked.

'An orienteering flag race,' Hilary replied. 'Four flags are going to be hidden in the woods tonight. Each team will be given a map this evening, which will have your flags marked on it. Tomorrow you will have to use the maps to find the flags. The team that gets back with all four of their flags first will be the winners.'

There was a buzz of excited chatter.

'The flag race thing sounds cool,' Jasmine said as the Owls rode back to the barn together.

Ahead of them the Bluejays were talking about the race too. 'I hope we win,' Lauren heard Paige say as they reached the barn.

'We will,' Kate declared in a very determined voice.

'Yeah, I hope,' Mel said.

'No, we *are* going to win,' Kate said.

'Yay! Go, Bluejays!' Allison exclaimed.
The others grinned. But Kate didn't.
Lauren saw Erin throw her a
questioning glance.

Kate's eyes flickered to one side as if
she had something she wanted to say in
private.

'Should we take Chess and Ziggy for
a walk down to the paddocks to cool
them off, Kate?' Erin said quickly.

Kate nodded and Lauren watched
them lead their ponies away. It was as if
they had some secret code. *That's pretty
strange*, Lauren thought.

★

That evening, as Lauren went to check on Twilight before dinner, she was surprised to find him pacing round his stable. 'Are you OK, boy?' she asked.

He stamped his foot and shook his head.

'What's the matter?' she said in alarm. 'You're not sick, are you?'

He shook his head again. Lauren felt relieved. 'What is it, then?'

Twilight nudged her with his nose. She felt frustrated. 'I don't know what it is. If only I could turn you into a unicorn!'

Twilight nodded.

Lauren looked at him in surprise. 'You want me too? But it's really risky!'

Twilight lifted a front hoof and stamped it down on the stable floor three times. Then he pushed her hard with his nose. He seemed very upset. Lauren's mind raced. She didn't want to break the camp rules but she knew Twilight wouldn't be asking her to turn him into a unicorn unless it was really urgent. She had to trust him. 'All right,' she agreed. 'I'll come back later tonight when everyone's at the campfire, OK?'

Twilight nodded.

Lauren gave him a hug. 'I'll get here as soon as I can,' she promised.

CHAPTER

Seven

The campfire was fun. They ate jacket potatoes and toasted marshmallows, but Lauren couldn't enjoy it completely. Her mind was on Twilight. What did he want? What was so urgent that he was prepared for her to take the risk and break camp rules by sneaking out to see him? As everyone started to sing 'Ten Green Bottles', Lauren slipped away.

The barn was dark inside but as the
door creaked open she heard Twilight
whinny.

Pulling the door shut behind her,
Lauren ran down the aisle and
whispered the Turning Spell. Purple light

lit up the air and Twilight turned into a unicorn.

Although it had only been a few days since she saw him in his magical form, it felt much longer. Lauren threw her arms round him. 'Oh, Twilight!' she exclaimed.

He whickered in delight. 'Hello, Lauren.'

'I've really missed seeing you as a unicorn,' she told him.

'I've really missed being one,' he replied. 'But I am enjoying camp.'

Lauren grinned. 'Me too. Especially now that I've made friends with Natasha, Julia, Rose and Jasmine.'

'Jasmine!' Twilight exclaimed as if remembering something. 'I've got to tell

you something about her. The reason
Nugget's been stopping when the jumps
get big is that Jasmine keeps dropping
the reins when they get near to the
fence. Nugget can jump small fences
without her having a contact with his
mouth but when the fences get bigger
he's losing confidence. You need to tell
her to keep hold of the reins and let her
hands follow his head when he goes
over the jump.'

'OK,' Lauren said quickly. 'So is that
why you wanted me to turn you into a
unicorn?'

'No,' Twilight said. 'I needed to talk to
you about Kate and Erin. I was in the
paddock this afternoon and I heard

them talking about the flag race. They've got a really mean plan to stop the Owls from winning.'

Lauren's eyes widened in shock. 'What are they going to do?' Then another thought struck her – a horrible one. 'Is Mel involved in the plan too?'

'No,' Twilight replied, to her relief. 'I heard Kate say that they mustn't tell Mel in case she tells you.'

'So what are they planning?' Lauren demanded.

But before Twilight could tell her they both heard the sound of footsteps approaching the barn and someone whistling.

'It's Tom!' Lauren gasped, recognizing the whistle.

'But I have to tell you what Kate and Erin are planning!' exclaimed Twilight.

'There isn't time,' Lauren said frantically. She began to say the words of the Undoing Spell quickly.

'Be careful tomorrow, Lauren. They're going to . . .'

But before Twilight could say anything else, Lauren reached the end of the spell and he turned back into a pony. It was just in time. The barn doors creaked open and Lauren crouched down in the darkness by Twilight's manger.

Holding her breath, and feeling very grateful that she'd shut the barn door so Tom wouldn't be suspicious, Lauren listened as he walked down the aisle.

Lauren's heart beat fast in her chest as the torch shone around. Would he look in Twilight's stall and see her? She saw him walk past and go into the tack room. When he came out he was carrying an armful of flags for the flag race the next day.

He walked up the aisle, still whistling softly.

As the doors shut behind him, Lauren's breath left her in a rush. 'I'd better go,' she whispered to Twilight.

He nodded but his eyes looked worried.

Giving him a quick kiss on the nose, she hurried out of the stall. She slipped out of the barn without anyone seeing her and set off across the grass. Lauren bit her lip. So Kate and Erin were planning something – something that would stop the Owls from winning. What could it be?

Twilight's words rang worryingly in her head. *Be careful tomorrow, Lauren. They're going to . . .*

What? Lauren thought. *What are they going to do?*

She reached the campfire just as the singsong ended and everyone started getting up to leave. She saw Mel. Would she have heard anything about the plan?

Just then, Mel glanced at her. As their eyes met, Mel gave a small smile. Lauren made up her mind. She went across. 'Hi,' she said awkwardly.

'Hi,' Mel replied.

'Do . . . do you want to walk back to the cabins together?' Lauren asked.

Mel nodded. Lauren's stomach felt

squirmy as they headed across the grass. She had to ask Mel about Kate. 'Um, Mel,' she began cautiously.

Mel looked at her quickly. 'Yes?'

Lauren realized that Mel probably thought she was about to apologize but right now she couldn't really think about their argument. There was something far more important to find out. 'Kate hasn't said anything about a plan for tomorrow, has she?' she asked.

Mel looked taken aback. 'Plan? What sort of plan?'

'To stop the Owls from winning,' Lauren answered.

'What are you talking about?' Mel asked, sounding mystified.

'I . . . I overheard something,' Lauren told her. 'I think she's planning something to stop the Owls from winning.'

'Don't be stupid!' Mel said in astonishment. 'Kate wouldn't do anything like that!'

'Well . . .' Lauren began.

'I don't believe you, Lauren!' Mel looked really angry. 'I thought you were going to say sorry but you're just making stuff up about Kate, aren't you? Just because you're jealous that I'm friends with her!'

'I'm not!' Lauren protested.

'Well, I can be friends with other people apart from you, you know!' Mel exclaimed. 'Leave me alone, Lauren, and stop making up mean things about Kate!' She marched away.

As Lauren stared after her, the unfairness of it all crashed down on her. She wasn't making it up! Why wouldn't Mel believe her?

Feeling angry with Mel and worried about the next day, she headed back to the cabin. When she got there, she found the other Owls getting ready for bed.

'I can't believe this is our last night here,' Jasmine said, as Lauren came in.

'Mmm,' Lauren said distractedly. Snatches of her argument with Mel kept coming back to her, mixing with Twilight's warning.

Be careful, Lauren . . .

What was Kate up to?

CHAPTER
Eight

'Right, guys, bring your ponies up to the jumping field with me,' Tom called the next morning.

Everyone began to follow him. All the ponies were groomed to perfection that day. No one had wanted to be responsible for their team losing marks. Not when it was the day that the winner of the cup would be decided.

Hilary had awarded all three teams ten points.

'I really hope Sinbad's OK in the woods,' Rose said nervously to Lauren.

'He'll be fine,' Lauren reassured her.

'We won't have to jump anything, will we?' Jasmine said. 'Nugget's bound to refuse if we do.'

'No, I don't think we'll have to jump,' Lauren replied. She remembered what Twilight had said the night before but she couldn't work out how to say anything to Jasmine. How could she explain that she knew why Nugget was refusing? *I'll think of a way*, she thought.

Tom handed each team a compass. The flags were marked on the maps with felt-tip pen; the Owls were collecting blue flags, Eagles green and Bluejays red.

'We need to go north up the mountain to get to the first flag,' Lauren said to her team as they looked at the map. 'Look, the contours are close together which means we have to go up a steep bit.'

'Yes, and it's by a stream,' Natasha pointed out.

'Remember, it's the first person back who wins, providing their team have collected all four flags,' Tom said. 'Are you ready?' He raised the whistle to his lips. 'Three, two, one . . . Go!'

The ponies plunged on. Lauren's

nerves faded away as she leant forward in the saddle and gave Twilight his head. They were off!

The three teams headed in different directions. The Owls galloped into the woods on a wide, sandy track. They charged along it, the ponies' hooves thudding on the soft ground. But as the path wound up the mountain it grew narrower and steeper and they had to slow down to a trot.

'The flag's got to be up here somewhere,' Lauren said, glancing at her map.

'Yes, we're heading north like the map says,' Julia said, looking at the compass.

The trees began pressing around them
and a stream appeared on their left-hand
side.

Sinbad began to spook and hang
back. Solitaire, Julia's pony, also began to
look nervous.

'It's very quiet here, isn't it?' Jasmine said.

Lauren nodded. The woods seemed to have closed around them, cutting them off from the rest of the camp. The trees seemed taller than the woods around her home, Granger's Farm. Lauren looked about her. When she was in the woods at home she always knew exactly where she was but here everything felt unfamiliar. *It would be so easy to get lost*, she thought. Twilight pulled anxiously at his bit. He seemed on edge too. He kept looking around as if he felt nervous about something. Lauren put a hand on his neck to try and reassure him.

'There!' Rose said suddenly.

She pointed to a fallen log at the side of the track. Sticking out of it was a blue flag.

Natasha pulled it out. 'Our first flag!' she cried triumphantly.

'Just three more to go,' Rose said.

They found the next flag fairly easily. The third flag was harder. Although they found the place where they thought it should be, they couldn't see it. They circled the area several times before Jasmine gasped and pointed up into a tree. It was hanging from one of the branches. 'There it is!'

Standing up in her stirrups, Lauren

pulled it down in a shower of leaves.
'We only need one more flag now!'
she exclaimed. This was fun!
Whatever it was that Kate and Erin
had been planning suddenly didn't
seem so important. They weren't
anywhere nearby, so what harm could
they do?

She and the others poured over the
map. It looked like the last flag was
further on up the mountain, near to a
footpath. A small hut had been marked
on the map and the flag symbol was
beside it.

'This way,' Lauren said, seeing that
they had to head east. She trotted down
the track and the others followed.

Keeping her eye on the map, Lauren led the way.

'There's the hut!' she cried excitedly, seeing a small bird–watchers' hide.

'The flag must be somewhere nearby,' Rose said.

But when they reached the hut they couldn't see the flag at all. They hunted inside and outside but there was no sign of it.

'Maybe there's another hut,' Jasmine suggested. 'Perhaps it's further up the mountain.' She pointed to a narrow path that led upwards.

'Maybe,' Lauren said, frowning at the map. 'But it looks like this hut is in the right place.'

'But the flag's not here,' Natasha said practically. 'We should go on further.'

They rode on. The track grew narrower and soon they were riding in single file.

'There don't seem to be any more huts,' Julia said.

'Let's just go on a bit further,' Rose urged.

They carried on, taking left turns and right turns. Lauren felt Twilight getting tenser and tenser and she began to worry. Was he nervous about them getting lost or was he just anxious because the woods were so different from their woods back at home? The trails in the woods around Granger's Farm were wide and sandy, whereas the paths they were on now were narrow and rocky underfoot, and covered over with a tangle of branches. *It's a shame we can't use Twilight's magic power to untangle the bushes!* Lauren thought as Twilight pushed his way gingerly past a long thorny bramble branch that grabbed at his neck and mane. Glancing down, she saw that they had ridden right off the edge of the map. 'Stop!' she exclaimed. 'This can't be right! We're not on the map any more.'

Once past the brambles, everyone halted. 'Look,' Lauren said, pointing it out on her map. 'I'm sure we rode past this fence about ten minutes ago. We must have gone the wrong way.'

'Oh no!' Natasha cried. 'Now we're definitely not going to win!'

'Yeah, and can anyone remember the way back?' Julia asked.

They looked at each other blankly.

'It can't be that hard to find,' Rose said. 'We just need to get back to where the map starts. We can use the compass to help us.'

But as she spoke, a deer bounded on to the path. It startled the ponies. Solitaire ran backwards in alarm and, in her struggle to grab her reins, Julia dropped the compass.

There was a crack as Sinbad stepped on it.

'Oh no!' Lauren gasped. Jumping off Twilight, she picked the compass up. It was broken!

'What are we going to do now?' Julia asked.

'I don't know,' Lauren said.

'We'll just have to try and follow the track back,' Natasha suggested.

They all nodded. But they'd only ridden a few minutes along the track when the track ended and they were faced with a choice of left or right.

'Left,' said Lauren.

'Right,' said Natasha.

'There were loads of turns like this!'

Jasmine wailed. 'How are we *ever* going to choose the right one?'

They looked at each other in panic. What were they going to do?

CHAPTER
Nine

'If we keep trying to guess our way home, we could end up really lost,' Rose said, looking worried.

Lauren touched Twilight's neck. A plan was forming in her mind. 'I know,' she said. 'You guys stay here and I'll ride up that track.' She nodded towards a very steep rocky track that led up the mountainside. 'If I get high enough, I might be able to look down on the valley. Then we'll have some idea of where we are and know which way to go.'

Natasha shook her head. 'We should stay together.'

'I'll only be gone five minutes – ten at most,' Lauren said. She saw the anxiety on their faces. 'Don't worry, I'll be fine. Twilight and I are used to the woods and we won't go far.'

'OK,' Rose said, frowning. 'But don't stay away too long.'

'I won't,' Lauren promised. 'Come on, Twilight.'

Twilight jogged eagerly up the track. She had a feeling he knew what she was planning.

As soon as they had gone a safe distance from the others, Lauren rode him into a clump of trees. 'I'm going to change you into a unicorn,' she whispered and, jumping off him, she said the Turning Spell.

She had never been more delighted to see him turn into a unicorn. 'Oh,

Twilight, what are we going to do?' she said anxiously.

'I thought this might happen,' Twilight said, looking worried. 'It's all Kate and Erin's fault. When I overheard them yesterday they were saying they were going to ride out very early this morning, find one of your blue flags and hide it. I knew it would be dangerous. I was sure you'd keep on trying to find it and end up lost.'

'Which is just what we have done,' Lauren groaned. 'Oh, Twilight, it might be ages before Hilary realizes we're lost. Even longer before she finds us.'

Twilight stepped forward to nuzzle her hair.

'What do you think we should do?'
Lauren said.

'Well, we could fly round and see
where we are from the air,' Twilight said,
considering the question. 'But someone
might see us.'

'We can't risk it,' Lauren told him.
She stepped through the trees and went
to the edge of the path to look down
the mountainside. As she did so, her foot
tripped on a rock that was half-covered
in brambles.

'Ow!' she cried, falling over.

'Look, Lauren!' Twilight gasped.

'What?' Lauren asked crossly as she
got to her feet. She'd been expecting a
bit more sympathy from him!

'The rock, Lauren!' Twilight exclaimed, staring at the rock Lauren had fallen over. 'It's made of rose quartz!'

Lauren stared at the pinky-grey rock. *Rose quartz!* 'You can use your horn to turn it into a magic mirror!' she said excitedly. 'Then we'll be able to see the whole mountainside and find our way back to camp!'

Twilight touched the rock with his horn. 'The mountainside,' he murmured.

Purple smoke appeared from nowhere and swirled over the rock. As it cleared, Lauren gasped with relief. In the rock's surface there was a moving picture of the mountainside laid out in front of them.

She could see the rest of the Owls waiting restlessly and the path twisting through the trees, and the hut where they had thought the flag should be.

'We just need to go a bit to the east,' she said, working out where they were. 'And then turn down the mountain, take two right turns and keep heading straight on. When we reach the hut it's easy, and we can go straight back to camp.' She could see a more direct path than the one they'd come up; it led through the pine trees. 'Oh, Twilight, now we'll be able to find our way home!'

She frowned as her eyes caught a movement in the trees on the map just near the hut. She leant closer and saw six ponies trotting out on to the path by the hut. 'It's the Bluejays!' she exclaimed. They had three red flags with them but were obviously still looking for one. They seemed to be arguing about which way to go.

They rode into the trees again. Lauren was about to stand up when her eyes caught a tiny flash of blue hidden in the thicket of trees near to where the Bluejays had just passed. She peered closer. 'Our missing flag!' she gasped. 'If we can get back to the hut and get it, we might still have a chance to beat the Bluejays and win the cup!'

'We can do it!' Twilight said excitedly. 'I know we can!'

Lauren said the Undoing Spell. The second he turned back into a pony she scrambled on to his back and they trotted down the trail.

Her friends were very relieved to see her. 'You're back!' Rose cried. 'We were getting worried about you.'

'Did you manage to see down the mountain?' Jasmine demanded.

'Er, sort of,' Lauren replied evasively. 'I think I know the way home, anyway.'

'Really?' Natasha said.

'Yes,' Lauren told her. She looked around at the others. 'Come on! Follow me!'

Twilight began to canter down the trail. Swept along by her confidence, the

others gathered up their reins and
cantered after her.

Lauren imagined the magic picture in
her mind. To the east, then right, right
again, then straight down the mountain,
take two rights and then straight on.
Her heart pounded in time with
Twilight's hooves thudding on the track.

'There's the hut!' Natasha exclaimed as they saw the bird-watchers' hut ahead of them.

Lauren remembered what she'd seen. 'There's a more direct route home,' she said, reining Twilight in. 'We just need to go through this thicket. If we can cut through it we'll find a path that takes us straight through the pine trees and back to camp!'

She headed into the thicket. There wasn't a proper path and Twilight had to twist and turn through the trees. *It would be much easier if we could fly!* Lauren thought. She grinned as she imagined how surprised her friends would be if they knew Twilight's secret. Suddenly her

eyes caught a glimpse of blue. 'The flag!'
she cried, realizing she was looking at a
corner of it sticking out from the
middle of a bush. Twilight trotted over
and pushed it with his nose. Pulling it
out of the bush, Lauren held it up.
'Look!' she cried. The others were
astonished.

'It's nowhere near where it said on
the map,' Jasmine said, checking. 'It's
definitely marked beside the hut.'

'That's a bit unfair,' Julia protested.
'Hilary and Tom should have put it
where they said they did on the map.'

'Maybe they did!' Jasmine gasped, her
eyes widening suddenly. 'Maybe someone
else moved it!'

The other Owls stared at her. Lauren held her breath. Would they work out what had happened?

'But who would have done something so mean?' Julia asked.

Lauren had to bite her tongue to stop herself from telling them.

'I bet it was the Bluejays,' Rose said

suddenly. 'You know how much they want to win.'

'It might not have been *all* of them,' Lauren said quickly. She didn't want Mel getting the blame.

'I wonder if they've won the race yet,' Rose said.

'There's only one way to find out,' Lauren cried. 'Let's get back there as quickly as we can!'

They began to canter. Suddenly Rose shrieked. 'Look!' She halted Sinbad so abruptly that they all almost bumped into her and pointed at a nearby tree. A red flag was leaning against it!

'One of the Bluejays' flags!' Lauren gasped.

'Let's hide it!' Jasmine said.

Lauren shook her head. 'No. We don't need to. Let's just get back to camp first and be the winners! That'll make them mad enough.'

'Yeah,' Rose said. 'Lauren's right. Come on!'

They continued down the trail. They hadn't gone far when they heard the sound of other ponies trotting through the trees to one side of them.

'Erin! Come on!' It was Kate's voice. 'The flag's got to be round here somewhere!'

'It's the Bluejays!' Natasha gasped. 'Quick, everyone!'

CHAPTER
Ten

As the Owls charged towards the camp they heard a faint yell of triumph in the woods behind them.

'They must've found the flag!' Jasmine exclaimed.

The Owls galloped down the trail as if it was a racetrack. Behind them, they could hear the faint drumming of hooves.

'They're coming after us!' Rose said.

'Don't worry!' Lauren called. 'We're almost out of the trees. Then there's just the field to gallop across and we're home.'

The track swung round a bend and they all shrieked. In front of them, a

pine tree had fallen across the track.
They pulled the ponies to a halt.

'We're going to have to jump it,'
Lauren said, glancing behind her.

'It should be OK,' Rose said. 'We
can jump the lower end. It's only the
size of the jumps we were doing in the
cross-country lesson.'

'But it's really wide!' Jasmine said
worriedly. 'Nugget will never jump it.'

Twilight whinnied. Lauren
remembered what he'd told her. 'Yes, he
will,' she said urgently to Jasmine. 'But
you need to keep a contact with his
mouth. I . . . I watched you the other
day when we were jumping,' she
invented. 'And when the jumps got big,

you dropped the reins every time you got a stride away from the jump. I bet if you keep a contact then he'll have the confidence to jump.'

'But I don't want to pull him in the mouth,' Jasmine protested.

'I know,' Lauren said. 'But you won't if you follow his head with your hands when he jumps.' She looked at Jasmine desperately. Behind them, she could hear shouts as the Bluejays got closer and closer. 'You can do it, Jasmine. I know you can! Just jump beside Twilight and me. We'll do the bigger side.'

Jasmine looked scared but nodded. 'OK,' she said, taking a deep breath.

With a whoop, Natasha set off for the

tree trunk. Rose and Julia followed close behind. One after another they flew over it. Lauren saw them waiting nervously on the other side for her and Jasmine.

'Ready?' Lauren said to Jasmine. Twilight gave Nugget's neck a comforting nudge. Lauren knew that if he'd been a unicorn he'd have been able to make courage flow into Nugget but even without his magic he still seemed to help. Nugget looked at him trustingly.

Jasmine shot Lauren an anxious look. For a moment Lauren thought she was going to say she'd changed her mind. But just then Kate and Erin came galloping round the corner with the other Bluejays close behind.

'Come on!' yelled Lauren. Twilight leapt into a canter and Nugget plunged alongside him.

They approached the tree trunk. Lauren suddenly realized that the bit of tree she was going to jump was very big – bigger than anything she'd ever jumped before. But she couldn't think about that now.

'Keep the contact!' she called to Jasmine as the ponies raced up to the log. They were four strides away, three strides . . .

Lauren saw Jasmine's hands start to drop.

'Hold on, Jasmine!' she cried.

Jasmine tightened her hold and the log was in front of them. Both ponies

pricked up their ears and sailed over it.
Twilight's jump was so big that Lauren
almost flew right out of the saddle, but
she grabbed his mane and managed to
stay on as he landed safely on the
other side.

'You did it!' she said happily to
Jasmine as they caught up to their
team-mates and galloped on.

Lauren heard a cheer. She thought it
was the other campers but then she
realized it was all the parents and the
camp counsellors. She remembered now
that all the parents were coming for a
barbecue on the final afternoon before
taking everyone home. They were all
watching from the finishing line.

'Come on!' yelled Natasha, as Kate came flying over the log behind them.

Leaning forward like a jockey, Lauren clapped her heels against Twilight's sides. They had to get across the finishing line first! Twilight raced on but she could hear the drumming of hooves on the grass behind her. Chess's black muzzle appeared alongside Twilight. Kate was leaning low over his withers, her face set and determined.

'Faster, Twilight!' Lauren gasped.

Flattening his ears, Twilight galloped even faster. Chess was fast and matched him stride for stride, but Twilight stretched every muscle in his body and went faster still. They began to draw away, one stride then two. Sticking his head out as far as it would go, Twilight swept under the finishing tape. He and Lauren had beaten Kate and Chess by a nose!

The crowd of watching parents and counsellors cheered and clapped. Lauren's breath rushed out in relief. They'd won the race! 'Oh, Twilight!' she gasped. 'You were fantastic!'

Pulling him up, she slid off his back. Her legs felt so shaky from the mad gallop that she had to hang on to the saddle to keep from collapsing in a heap. Within seconds the other Owls had galloped up beside her. 'We won!' Rose cried.

'I know!' Lauren exclaimed.

'Not just the race but the cup as well!' Rose said.

'We've beaten the Bluejays!' Julia told her.

'Twilight was awesome!' Natasha declared.

'Oh, Lauren!' Jasmine said. 'That was so exciting!'

'You jumped the log,' Lauren said to her.

'Yeah!' Jasmine's eyes shone. 'And it felt amazing!'

Someone came pushing through them. It was Mel. She was leading Shadow and her face was glowing. 'Oh, Lauren! You were brilliant!'

'Thanks!' Lauren grinned.

The others began to move away to say hi to their parents.

Mel looked at Lauren. 'I'm really glad you won, you know.' There was a strange note to her voice. 'Some really mean stuff went on today. I didn't know about it till we were out doing the race but you were right, Kate and Erin were trying to stop your team from winning. They . . . they moved one of your flags. I found out just now when we were riding through the woods. I'm sorry that I didn't believe you.' She hesitated. 'Are we still friends?'

'Of course we are,' Lauren told her. 'Best friends.'

Mel smiled happily.

Hilary clapped her hands. 'OK, everyone. The barbecue will be starting in ten minutes. We'll be presenting the prizes then. But I can tell you that the winner of the team cup for the week is . . .' she paused, 'the Owls team!'

There was a burst of applause. Twilight pushed Lauren with his nose and she grinned in delight.

As the applause died down she gave him a kiss on the nose.

'Mum's over there,' Mel said, waving. 'I'm going to go and say hello.'

Lauren was just about to follow her when Jasmine came bursting out of the crowd. 'Lauren! Lauren! Guess what?'

'What?' Lauren asked in astonishment.

'My mum and dad said that I can have a pony!' Jasmine said. 'They saw me jump that log and they were so impressed at how much my riding's improved this week, they've said I can get a pony of my own now!'

'That's great!' Lauren cried.

'It's all down to you,' Jasmine grinned. 'You helped me jump it!' She hugged her. 'Thanks, Lauren. I couldn't have done it without you.' She glanced over her shoulder. 'I've got to find Julia and tell her too!' She raced off, a smile stretching across her face from ear to ear.

Lauren felt as she was floating on air. 'Isn't that great, Twilight?' she said. 'I can't believe we thought we were going to have a whole week without magic. It hasn't turned out like that at all! We've helped lots of people even though we've been here at camp.'

Twilight whickered in delight.

Lauren looked round at the busy camp, thronged with people. It had been a brilliant five days. She hoped she could come back again next year! Just then Rose, Natasha, Jasmine, Julia and Mel came charging up to her with their ponies. 'Lauren!' Natasha cried. 'The barbecue's starting!'

'There's ice cream!' Rose put in.

'And a huge barrel of carrots for the ponies!' Mel said.

'Twilight deserves the most,' Jasmine added. 'He's amazing!'

Lauren grinned to herself. 'Yes,' she agreed, 'he is.'

Meeting her gaze, Twilight snorted cheekily.

'Come on, Lauren!' Mel urged as
Lauren hugged him.

'I'm coming,' Lauren smiled. Then,
chattering and laughing together, she and
the others led the ponies over to join in
the fun.